The Contemporary Composers

MICHAEL TIPPETT

The Contemporary Composers

Series Editor: Nicholas Snowman

MICHAEL TIPPETT

Meirion Bowen

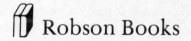 Robson Books

Other titles available in The Contemporary Composers
series

Peter Maxwell Davies by Paul Griffiths
Gyorgy Ligeti by Paul Griffiths
Harrison Birtwistle by Michael Hall

FIRST PUBLISHED IN GREAT BRITAIN IN HARD-
BACK IN 1982 BY ROBSON BOOKS LTD., BOLSOVER
HOUSE, 5-6 CLIPSTONE STREET, LONDON W1P
7EB. THIS ROBSON PAPERBACK EDITION FIRST
PUBLISHED IN 1985. COPYRIGHT © 1982 MEIRION
BOWEN

British Library Cataloguing in Publication Data
Bowen, Meirion
    Michael Tippett. – (The Contemporary composers)
    1. Tippett, Michael
    I. Title II. Series
    780'.92'4   ML410.T467
    ISBN 0-86051-282-7

Printed in Hungary

CONTENTS

Acknowledgements

I am indebted, first and foremost, to the composer for allowing me to probe and test him out with irritating persistence on many items related to his life and work. Whilst aware that he considers critical studies of his work to be directed at people other than himself, I trust he will nevertheless think this book to have been worthy of his interest and collaboration.

I should like to thank the staff at Schott & Co. Ltd. for their constant help and encouragement, and especially Sally Groves and Alan Woolgar, for keeping me abreast of new information, scores and publications relevant to my task. All Tippett's music is published by Schott & Co. Ltd. and the musical examples here are reproduced with their kind permission.

I am grateful to Faber & Faber Ltd., for their permission to reproduce excerpts from Murray Schafer's interview with Tippett in *British Composers in Interview*; to the University of Texas at Austin, for permission to include excerpts from Tippett's 1976 Doty lectures in Fine Art; *Quarto Magazine* for permission to reprint Tippett's review of Shostakovich's *Testimony*, and Hamish Hamilton for permission to quote from the latter volume.

This book would not have reached completion in its present form without the stimulus that came from my consultations with various individuals. In particular, I am much indebted to Ian Kemp and Alan Woolgar for keeping an eye open for factual errors. I have benefited much, too, from heated argument with Symon Clarke.

Finally, I should like to thank Laurie Coombs for finding time to type the entire book, in between making arrangements for the Reading Rock Festival.

TO JONN LEEDHAM

. . . You ask the secret.
It has just one name:
again.

Miroslav Holub   *Ode to Joy*

EDITOR'S PREFACE

It is no secret that our epoch favours a museological rather than a prospective approach to musical activity. Such a situation is, of course, the reflection of a cultural climate, but it is also the result of problems particular to the evolution of musical language during this century.

Whatever the fundamental causes, the effects are clear. The repertoire of 'classical' music has been extended backwards in time and enlarged with the inclusion of many important works as well as a great number of lesser ones. At the same time the 'standard' works of the eighteenth and nineteenth centuries have become more than ever entrenched in a musical world very largely conditioned by market considerations and thus inimical to contemporary endeavour. One cannot blame record company employees, concert promoters and artists' agents for being more interested in quick turnover than in the culture of their time. The results are inevitable: re-recordings of the same symphonies and operas multiply; performances of the same 'early' music, claiming to be less inauthentic than their rivals, abound; and conductors' careers are made with an ever-diminishing bunch of scores.

Where does this leave the music written yesterday and today? The answer is not encouraging. As far as western Europe and the United States are concerned, contemporary works inhabit a number of well defined ghettos.

In West Germany it is the radio stations that commission

and perform new scores and, naturally enough, their concern is to satisfy their specialist listeners rather than to cultivate a wider public. Except for a certain number of important but brief 'shop window' festivals, contemporary music is hardly a living affair.

In the United States composers find sanctuary in the universities—comfort and security but little contact with the general musical public outside the walls. And in times of economic regression, enterprising and excellent modern music ensembles encounter increasing financial difficulties, whilst symphony orchestras, reliant for their existence on the whims of the rich and generally conservative, play safer than ever.

In the UK, outside the BBC and one or two imaginative enterprises like Glasgow's Musica Nova, the situation is depressing—on the one hand, inadequate state funds spread too thinly, on the other, excellent but hungry orchestras competing for the same marketable fodder. Britain, in spite of at least two recent determined attempts, cannot even boast a modest but representative contemporary music festival worthy of international attention.

France, with its rigorous but narrow education system giving little place to the non-literary arts, has suddenly in these last few years woken up to the charms of music and begun to invest more and more heavily in this new passion. Though it will take years before this musically rootless country can boast the proliferation of performing talent of its neighbours, native respect for the 'intellect' ensures that the music of today is discussed, played and subsidized relatively correctly. Yet in spite of all the activity, contemporary music outside Paris attracts small audiences; the work of 'decentralization' so dear to Gallic politicians is more arduous here than in other countries.

This is not the place for a thorough survey of the status of contemporary music in the world in general. However, it seems clear that even a brief glance at a few different countries reveals the existence of an uneasy relationship between the contemporary public and its music. Certainly, a few independently minded and cultivated musicians seek by their artistic policies to persuade the musical public to accept the endeavours of the present as well as the rich and varied musical traditions and structures of the past.

This new series of books, each introducing a different living composer, seeks to supplement the work of the pathfinders. The scope of the series does not reflect any particular musical 'party line' or aesthetic; its aims are to be representative of what exists, and to supply the listener who stumbles across a new piece at a Prom or on record with the essential facts about its composer—his life, background and work.

London, June 1981   NICHOLAS SNOWMAN

INTRODUCTION

'You say,' wrote William Blake to the Reverend Dr John Trusler, author of *The Way to be Rich and Respectable*, 'that I want somebody to Elucidate my Ideas. But you ought to know that What is made Explicit to the Idiot is not worth my care . . . But I am happy to find a Great Majority of fellow Mortals who can Elucidate my Visions and Particularly they have been Elucidated by Children, who have taken a greater delight in contemplating my Pictures than I even hoped.'

Sir Michael Tippett could certainly echo Blake's words. He too has had to deal with the musical counterpart to Dr Trusler —the patron who only wants what he knows, who is unresponsive, even indignant, when presented with anything fresh, singular or extraordinary. Fortunately for Tippett, today's young generation seem to find his work easier to elucidate than did their predecessors. They are, of course, at an advantage. Most of Tippett's compositions are now written. His *oeuvre*—even though he may well add to it some major pieces in the next ten, fifteen or (hopefully) twenty-five years—can be considered as a whole. Most of it is also recorded. Back in the Forties and Fifties an older generation had only a small number of works available for consideration and few recordings. They can be forgiven for not estimating Tippett at his true worth, or for not sensing his potential. Nevertheless, Tippett remains 'the most loved and least analysed of our great composers'—as one tribute to him in his seventy-fifth year maintained.*

As far as I know, this book is the first attempt to consider all of Tippett's music in some depth. Its scope is still limited but precise within the aims of the series. Ian Kemp, who edited an excellent sixtieth birthday symposium on Tippett—long out-of-print, unfortunately—now has an authorized biography on the near horizon. This will investigate the composer's life and intellectual development at far greater length than I can afford here: and it will offer as much space to individual works as I can muster for Tippett's entire output.

Thus, here, I have sketched in only the essential features of Tippett's life and concentrated on his musical development. I have also confined myself as far as possible to the major works, only managing to mention in passing such delightful pot-pourris as the Suite for the Birthday of Prince Charles (Suite in D) and the *Divertimento: Sellinger's Round*.

I start (in ''Tis Nature's Voice') from the point at which Tippett managed to crystallize his ideas on the relationships between words and music, especially in a dramatic context. I then consider the oratorio, *A Child of Our Time* and the four operas. All subsequent sections stem from these. The rest of the book contains photographs, the answers Tippett has given in various interviews on more general aspects of composition, and also some comments on the cultural scene—general and specific. Finally, there are a list of compositions and recordings, a bibliography, and glossary of technical terms.

The book is only a beginning, but it may enable some of the composer's fellow Mortals to Elucidate his Visions.

July 1981   M.B.

* Andrew Clements in *Music and Musicians*, January 1980, p. 14.

1 INNOCENCE AND EXPERIENCE

IN HIS MIDDLE SEVENTIES, Sir Michael Tippett has come to be regarded as one of the foremost living composers. Such recognition occurred quite late. His achievement was long underestimated. On the other hand, Tippett was never a prodigy: only gradually did he reach maturity as a composer. Born in London, on 2 January 1905, he had little opportunity to acquire an appropriate musical training and experience until he left school. Even after he had left the Royal College of Music, it was at least seven more years—including a period of further tuition—before he found his feet and began to produce works which bore his own discernible imprint.

None of Tippett's immediate family was musical. His father, Henry William Tippett (1858–1944) was a lawyer who retired early, having successfully invested in some business enterprises, including the Lyceum Theatre in London. His mother, Isabel Clementine Binny Kemp (1880–1969) trained as a nurse. Although they were from the well-to-do middle class, both parents espoused non-Establishment views and opinions. Tippett's father was a Manchester liberal and rationalist; his mother was a novelist, Labour party member, suffragette (for which she went to prison), do-gooder and general supporter of worthy causes. They coped more easily with their elder son, Peter (b. 1904)—who was to distinguish himself in the navy—than with young Michael, whose musical ambitions left them bemused. Neither they nor their son had any well-formed notions as to what a musical career might entail, let alone what a budding composer should do to fulfil his creative longings.

The year Michael Tippett was born, the family moved from Eastcote in Middlesex to a house in the village of Wetherden, Suffolk. Away from the London concert scene, Tippett remained largely innocent of music during his childhood. His mother sang him drawing-room ballads by Quilter and others. He himself enjoyed taking part in the hymns and anthems in the local church choir. One day a young girl walked past the cottage singing 'Everybody's doing it'. This tune stuck in his mind. So did the songs he heard sung by young men marching off to the First World War. Tippett was only later to learn what these songs meant. Meanwhile, no radio, records or tapes existed to provide him with any alternative musical experience.

When he was nine, Tippett's parents sent him to a pre-paratory school in Dorset. After that, he proceeded to a public school near Edinburgh. His stay there was nasty, brutish and short. He found the bullying, the homosexuality and the emphasis on cold baths in winter quite intolerable. He asked his parents to take him away. They did so, promptly. While they were about it, they encouraged the elderly headmaster in his plans for retirement.

Tippett then went to Stamford Grammar School in Lincoln-shire. This was more congenial. Inspired by some teachers in particular, he excelled in science subjects and history. He also argued his way out of organized religion and the cadet corps. Meanwhile, because of financial difficulties, his parents went to live at an hotel they owned at Cannes in the South of France. Tippett often spent his vacations with them, travelling out on his own. He became fluent in French as a result. The rest of the time, he fended for himself. That he enjoyed. Confident of his own intellectual brilliance, he engaged in polemic with all his teachers. Delighted to be independent, he followed his own whims and fancies. The money his parents gave him to buy clothes he saved for his own devices. An interfering aunt made him buy a bowler hat, cane and gloves, but he threw these into the sea at Marseilles. At the same time as he abandoned God, he took to marmalade, having discovered its restorative powers during many arduous journeys to visit his parents. To this day, it has remained his chief balm and solace in times of stress or crisis.

During his Stamford days, Tippett's musical appetite was further whetted, but never properly satisfied. For patriotic reasons, music—together with other 'inessential' subjects, such as horse-riding—was excluded during wartime from the school curriculum. Tippett managed to have piano lessons with a local teacher, Mrs Tinkler, and came to know some of the Beethoven piano sonatas. When he was fourteen, he was taken to an orchestral concert in Leicester, conducted by Malcolm Sargent. Enthralled by what he heard—especially Ravel's suite, *Mother Goose*—he set his mind on becoming a composer. Thereafter, nothing would stand in his path. When his parents agreed to remove their disruptive son from Stamford, the headmaster, on learning from the boy that he would make his career as a composer, opined that Tippett would never earn enough to afford a boiled egg, let alone a boiled shirt. His Stamford lodgings were immediately placed out of bounds to other boys, also, in case his atheism turned into an epidemic.

Tippett began to teach himself to compose. He bought Charles Stanford's *Musical Composition*. One sentence early on in the book left an indelible impression. 'The first principle to be laid down is . . . to *study counterpoint first, and through counterpoint to master harmony.*'[1] Instinctively, Tippett knew that this method was right for him and so sought mastery first and foremost as a contrapuntal composer.

Then, a chance encounter with a professional musician on a train opened his parents' eyes to the existence of the Royal College of Music. On condition that Tippett would aim to become a Doctor of Music, they agreed to pay their son's fees for a period of study there. An interview with the College Principal, Sir Hugh Allen, was arranged. Tippett was admitted—largely, he now thinks, because his mother smiled charmingly at Sir Hugh—and attended for the first time in the summer of 1923. This was his first encounter with the world of professional music.

Already, when Tippett went to the RCM, his aspirations were

17

Olympian, though his knowledge rudimentary. He studied briefly with Charles Wood, who showed him some of the formal subtleties of Beethoven's music. Tippett chose not to continue his studies with Vaughan Williams—for he did not want to become another VW imitator, as others were (e.g. Gordon Jacob, Imogen Holst and Elizabeth Maconchy). Instead, he enrolled with an avowed arch-pedant, Dr C. H. Kitson. Mutual agony ensued. Over the next five years, venerable professors like Kitson were continually to shake their heads in disbelief at the notion of Tippett entering upon a musical career. Nevertheless, Tippett persevered. He acquired a general musical education by going to concerts—especially the Proms, where he heard all the Beethoven symphonies for the first time. Curious to know what sixteenth-century music sounded like, he attended services at Westminster Cathedral, copying out in advance from library scores the Palestrina masses and so on that were to be sung. He went a lot to the theatre, discovering Chekhov, Ibsen, Strindberg and, above all, Shaw. He read voraciously. He taught himself German, partly for musical purposes, but also in order to read Goethe. He embarked on Frazer's *The Golden Bough* and Gibbon's *Decline and Fall.*

At the RCM, he learnt the piano with Aubin Raymar. He also studied conducting with Sargent, who appeared frighteningly superior, but was actually quite practical. Sargent set about equipping pupils like Tippett with the sort of techniques that are useful in rehearsing and performing with amateurs: anything else, he felt, would be outside their scope. Kindest of all Tippett's teachers was Adrian Boult. He allowed Tippett to sit beside him on the rostrum at the First Orchestra rehearsals every Friday afternoon for four years. Thus, 'Boult's darling', as he was called, became familiar with many standard classics and with works like Wagner's *Parsifal*. Tippett also sang in some unusual new compositions, such as Vaughan Williams's *Sir John in Love* and Holst's *Hymn of Jesus*. He failed his final examinations at the first attempt, but eventually graduated with a Bachelor of Music degree in 1928.

From now on, Tippett made composition the main focus of his existence. He lived at almost subsistence level and confined whatever musical and teaching work came his way to the minimum. Creative endeavours were his first priority. For a while he continued living in London; this included a short period at the East End mission for the poor run by Haileybury School, which made him uneasy, for his involvement in social work often left him with little energy for composition. Then he was invited to conduct a concert and operatic society promoted by the Oxted and Limpsfield Players; he combined this with a madrigal group (mainly to explore the madrigal repertoire for himself), and managed to rent a tiny cottage on a farm in Oxted. Later, his father gave him enough money to have a modern bungalow built near the cottage.

Life was spartan. Tippett collected wood and built his own fires; he ate lunch at the farm but otherwise fed himself. He had to make his own marmalade, and once nearly set the house on fire in the process. Nevertheless, he was composing, avidly. He managed some enterprising productions with the local society, including Vaughan Williams's *The Shepherds of the Delectable Mountains*, Stanford's *The Travelling Companion* and Tippett's own version of the eighteenth-century ballad opera, *The Village Opera*. He directed a complete performance (a rarity, then) of Handel's *Messiah*, introducing each part, explaining its shape and contents: this, too, proved important for himself as a composer, for later he used *Messiah* as a model for his oratorio, *A Child of Our Time*.

On 5 April 1930, the first concert of Tippett's own music took place—an entire programme of first performances directed by a former fellow-student, David Moule Evans, in the Barn Theatre at Oxted. It included Tippett's Concerto in D, for flutes, oboes, horns and strings; Three Songs; *Jockey to the Fair*, for piano; a String Quartet in F; and Psalm in C, for chorus and orchestra, a setting of *The Gateway* by Christopher Fry. (Tippett himself designed the programme, and absent-mindedly omitted his own name.) A review of the concert in *The Times* two days later said that Tippett's music had 'a personal distinction and sincerity which is absent from the work of the Central European composers of today': a comment that reveals not so much discernment as a parochialism of

19

outlook similar to that which prevented the young Benjamin Britten at this time from going abroad to study with Alban Berg. A *Daily Telegraph* review also expressed enthusiasm, but suggested that 'Michael Tippett will probably prefer to put all behind him and go on to fresh ideas . . .'

Tippett did precisely that. As far as he was concerned, the concert revealed distinct limitations in his technique. He therefore withdrew these works and decided to undertake further study, which was arranged, through the Royal College of Music, with R. O. Morris. Firmly, but sympathetically, Morris guided him through sixteenth-century counterpoint and fugue in the style of Bach. The going was hard, but Tippett responded and his grasp of the linear and formal aspects of music was thereby strengthened.

At this time, Tippett did some part-time teaching—French, not music—at Hazelwood Preparatory School, Limpsfield, where he met and became a close friend of Christopher Fry. He gave up this teaching in 1932 to take charge of music at work-camps near Boosbeck, a small mining village in Cleveland, Yorkshire. These camps were created to help unemployed ironstone miners survive by developing their own land economy and local culture. Tippett directed performances at Boosbeck of *The Beggar's Opera* and his own folk-song opera, *Robin Hood*, with local villagers taking part.

During his student days and after, Tippett had become aware of events in the world at large. He learnt about the harsh realities of the First World War. He mixed with trade unionists and with members of left-wing youth organizations modelled on the socialist *Wandervogel* movements in Germany. He acquired first-hand experience of the Depression and unemployment. Hiking up into the North of England, he saw 'for the first time, with horrified eyes, the undernourished children. When I returned to the well-fed South, I was ashamed.'[2]

Although he was aware that composition would entail a life of isolation and independence from the world, Tippett was 'quite certain that . . . somewhere music could have a direct relation also to the compassion that was so deep in my own heart'. His music-making at this time was thus closely linked to

20

his politics. He organized the South London Orchestra, formed from musicians thrown out of their work in cinemas by the arrival of talkies. They gave concerts in colleges, theatres, school halls, parks and churches in South London. The repertory consisted mainly of popular classics, but Tippett sometimes introduced novelties such as Stravinsky's Violin Concerto (which, as a composer, he wanted to get to know). He also directed two choirs sponsored by the Royal Arsenal Co-operative Society, initially performing songs of a political nature, though later they embarked upon light opera. When they performed for the poor of London's East End, Tippett arranged that each of them should bring *two* meals, so that they could feed themselves and the audience. In this period, Tippett was a Trotsky sympathizer and he joined the Communist Party for a few months in 1935: but he left when he failed to convert his party branch to Trotskyism. His radicalism was absolute and deeply passionate. He wrote an anti-capitalist play, *War Ramp*, which was performed at various Labour Party rallies: *War Ramp* foreshadows Joan Littlewood's *Oh! What A Lovely War*. Tippett at this time even advocated revolution by violent means, but his active participation in Trotskyism began to wane when he saw that none of it seemed powerful enough to answer the barbarities of Nazism or Stalinism. Unlike his composer-colleague, Alan Bush, who has remained one of the Stalinist faithful right up to the present day, Tippett now detached himself from political involvement.

Meanwhile, he had composed a String Quartet in A, which was included in a programme of chamber music by the Brosa Quartet at the Mercury Theatre, London, in December 1935. Although he later revised the piece—substituting a new first movement for the original first *two* movements—he felt that it was here that his own personal voice was being heard for the first time. He was not so happy with some other works from this period, and suppressed them. These included a Symphony in B flat (whose first movement was rehearsed and performed by the London Symphony Orchestra under the composer's baton, at a Royal College of Music Patron's Fund concert in 1935); a setting of Blake's *Song of Liberty* and a children's opera,

Robert of Sicily. After the String Quartet No. 1 (as it became) he wrote a series of compositions all of which were to attain eventual performance and publication, marking the entry on to the musical scene of a composer of distinct achievement: these included, notably, the Piano Sonata No. 1 (1936/7) and the Concerto for Double String Orchestra (1938/9).

In the Twenties and Thirties, Tippett had accumulated a variety of friends, inside and outside the musical profession. None was more crucial to the crystallization of his work and career than the poet T. S. Eliot. Tippett has described in detail the circumstances of his meetings with Eliot, whom he calls his 'spiritual father'.[3] Their discussions led Tippett to a more precise formulation of his ideas regarding the relationships between words and music, especially in the context of oratorio and opera. This occurred at a time when he was moving towards some kind of statement of his position as a creative artist in an increasingly strife-torn world. While many radicals of the time rushed off to Spain during the Civil War, and aimed their attacks on governments and the economic institutions, Tippett was more conscious of the presence of social outcasts in societies in general. He looked for some time for an opportunity to express his compassion towards such outcasts. When the chance arrived, he was lucky enough to have Eliot's guidance and encouragement in producing his enduring creative response: *A Child of Our Time*.

In 1938, the shooting of a German diplomat by a young Polish Jew, made desperate by the Nazi persecution of his race in general and of his family in particular led to one of the most terrible pogroms of Jews in central Europe. Tippett shared in the public horror which this aroused. He felt inwardly he must answer it with a composition embodying that response. To that end he changed what was going to be an opera about the Easter Rebellion in Ireland into an oratorio for which, on Eliot's advice, he wrote his own text. To produce both text and music involved him in the arduous process of selecting from a great accretion of images—from Blake, Wilfred Owen, Jung (whom he had recently read), and other sources. It also meant simplifying the musical content to enable it to tell powerfully at every stage. Much of the same process was to recur when, in later years, he wrote his four operas. But here it was a new experience: one that taught Tippett a lot—more, in fact, than might be apparent in the final work itself. In writing the oratorio he came to see clearly that he must reject all ideological commitment, detach himself from the immediacies of present conflict and develop a type of artistic expression that stood for deeper values. Instead of just protesting, he concentrated on demonstrating the power of compassion, tolerance, love and forgiveness. These values shine through all his mature work.

A Child of Our Time was also connected with Tippett's own personal turmoil in this period. Three friends had become especially close to him—Wilfred Franks, Evelyn Maude and Francesca Allinson. With the last of these he even contemplated marriage; but this could not work. Under considerable strain from the respective pressures of these relationships, Tippett consulted an analyst, the Jungian, John Layard; he continued his own self-analysis thereafter. But it was only through the special effort of composition that Tippett could engineer a reconciliation of the 'shadow' and the 'light' within himself. The sense of wholeness and integrity sought after and attained by the oratorio were evidently as necessary for the composer as an individual as they were to society at large.

A Child of Our Time prophesies the horrors and social consequences of war. Likewise, Tippett's espousal of the pacifist cause was as much the outcome of this insight as it was a reaction to the war as such. Tippett joined the Peace Pledge Union in 1940 (it had been founded five years earlier by the Reverend Dick Sheppard), and registered as a conscientious objector. Three years later, he was sentenced to three months' imprisonment for failing to comply with the conditions of registration (i.e. to undertake non-combatant military duties, work at a farm, or a hospital, or teach in a civil defence establishment). Tippett would brook no compromise on the issue. By composing, teaching and directing musical performances, he felt that he was serving a cause no less moral than that which he might uphold by fighting for the allies. Vaughan

Williams was amongst those who spoke at his trial, but to no avail. On 21 June 1943, Tippett was taken to Wormwood Scrubs, handcuffed to an army deserter; his immediate neighbours in the prison were a rapist and a murderer. Tippett's mother, some years later, declared it her 'proudest moment' when her son went to prison. The composer himself said he felt he had 'come home'. At the Scrubs, he sewed mail-bags, not very efficiently, and took charge of a tiny orchestra. When Peter Pears and Benjamin Britten visited the prison to give a recital, Tippett contrived to assist in page-turning, even though they had brought John Amis for the purpose.

Already a thin man, Tippett became even thinner on prison diet. He found it difficult to concentrate on reading. Above all, he was bursting to compose. His letters to Evelyn Maude at this time[4] speak of the symphony that was gestating inside him. On his release—one month early, due to good behaviour—he attended a small celebration and a performance of his Second String Quartet, and then went for a short holiday in Cornwall with some friends. There, he narrowly escaped a further term of imprisonment when a coastguard apprehended them all bathing in the nude.

Tippett's reputation as a composer had meanwhile grown steadily, even though only a few pieces of his had received professional performances, and the BBC, ISCM Festival and the publishers Boosey and Hawkes had all turned down works like the Double Concerto. In May 1939, Tippett had attended a performance of Hindemith's *Mathis der Maler* at the Queen's Hall, London. During the interval he was introduced to Willy Strecker, the director of Schott's music publishing firm in Mainz. Strecker asked to see a representative selection of his work. Tippett obliged. Just after the outbreak of war, he received a reply which stated that Schott would publish the First Piano Sonata and Double Concerto. In the event, Tippett's works were published by Schott in London. The first to appear in print (in 1942) were the Piano Sonata No. 1 and the *Fantasia on a Theme of Handel* (written between 1939 and 1941). Later, in 1944, *A Child of Our Time* was published. This was the first of Tippett's works to attract attention and praise outside England. Tippett has remained with Schott ever since.

When the war started, adult education was suspended. Tippett's RACS choirs were disbanded and he returned briefly to Hazelwood School to teach classics. But then in 1940, he was invited by Eva Hubback, the principal of Morley College, to become Director of Music there. A bomb had recently hit and badly damaged the building. Classes were moved to a nearby school. Nevertheless, during the next eleven years, Tippett gave Morley College a new lease of life, musically. He attracted onto the staff a number of important musical refugees from central Europe. They included the composer Matyas Seiber, the musicologist Walter Bergmann, the conductor Walter Goehr and three string players who were later to join forces with a fourth (English) player to form the Amadeus Quartet. Tippett discovered the counter-tenor Alfred Deller in Canterbury Cathedral and brought him to Morley to sing the important solos in Purcell's Odes. He organized and took part in a variety of performances—from the first complete Monteverdi *Vespers* to Stravinsky's *Les Noces* and Frank Martin's *Le Vin Herbé*. The Morley Choir, which most of the time Tippett himself directed, were especially successful in contemporary works and in pre-classical music. One project—Tallis's 40-part motet, *Spem in Alium*—which took two years to rehearse properly, later led to a recording of the work.[5] And when, years later, Walter Legge wanted a chorus-master for his newly formed Philharmonia Chorus, he turned first to Tippett—who rejected the offer, as it would have been too great a distraction from composition.

At this time (1942) Tippett became friendly with Benjamin Britten and Peter Pears. They had recently returned from the USA, where they had spent the early years of the war. They appeared at Morley College concerts and sometimes stayed with Tippett at Oxted. In 1943, Tippett wrote for them a cantata for voice and piano, *Boyhood's End*—a piece that reflected their common interest in Purcell. Britten also expressed enthusiasm for *A Child of Our Time* and urged Tippett to arrange a performance. This came about, eventually, on 19 March 1944 at the Adelphi Theatre in London. Pears was one of the four soloists. *The Times* reviewed it, favourably. Performances in Holland and Germany followed, partly through Howard Hartog, who was then working for Hamburg Radio (then in allied hands) and who was later to join the staff at Schott's in London.[6] The impact of the oratorio on the continent was profound. Oddly, the work was banned until very recently in Israel, because the text mentioned the name *Jesus*.

Tippett and Britten were rarely so close after the première of Britten's opera, *Peter Grimes*, in 1945. Britten was moving into an altogether different creative stratum and saw himself primarily as an opera composer. Tippett wanted to diversify his compositional efforts and certainly wanted to avoid becoming a mere satellite of the phenomenally gifted younger composer. Some rivalry—even if it were unconscious rivalry—was inevitable. But Britten's meteoric rise did not cause Tippett the neurotic insecurity it provoked in some of his contemporaries, who resented the prominence of Aldeburgh in English musical life. Tippett went his independent way. Right up until Britten's death in 1976, the two composers remained fervent friends, with the deepest respect for each other's attainments.[7]

After the war, Tippett continued living at Oxted, frugally as ever. He began to limit his Morley work and other commitments as he wanted more time for composition. He also started giving talks on the BBC Third Programme and World Service. These provided him with a modest secondary income. Thus, in 1951, he decided to resign from Morley College—though not before he had conducted the choir in a performance as part of the Festival of Britain.

By this time, Tippett had written his First Symphony; Sargent conducted the première in Liverpool, in 1945. Also, in 1946, the Zorian Quartet had given the first performance of his Third String Quartet. But Tippett's main obsession now was the opera he wanted to write, *The Midsummer Marriage*. This he began in 1946, at first collaborating on the libretto with the poet, Douglas Newton, but then continuing on his own. For the next six years it dominated his whole existence. He had no idea whether it would ever reach the operatic stage. He composed it out of sheer inner necessity. It became an act of faith and of tremendous self-discipline. Often he was exhausted. Once he fell so ill, he thought he had cancer. Composition has always given Tippett a curious kind of psychosomatic discomfort. In his youth and middle age he could rarely afford the holidays that would enable him to switch off completely and forget the compositional obsession. Creating opera on the scale of *The Midsummer Marriage* was thus the greatest labour he could ever endure.

Tippett moved in 1951 to a large, leaky, tumbledown manor in Wadhurst, Sussex. His mother joined him there (his father having died in 1944), but their life-styles were often discordant. She kept all the windows open in winter. He wanted them closed against the cold and built roaring fires. She kept her part of the garden in fastidious order. He allowed his to run wild. She had long since been a vegetarian. He liked a varied diet. She was much influenced by the ideas of Rudolf Steiner and took to faith-healing. She also maintained her belief in laxatives, alarming her son by sometimes mixing them into the main course for dinner when they had guests. Interestingly, Tippett's mother had, in her seventies, taken up painting. Her work is dominated by religious themes symbolically presented.

During this post-war period, Tippett allowed few other projects to distract him from *The Midsummer Marriage*. He did take time off to fulfil a BBC commission—a Suite for the Birthday of Prince Charles, in 1948, whose first performance was given under the direction of Boult. Tippett also completed in 1950–51 the song-cycle, *The Heart's Assurance*. This was his long-considered memorial to Francesca Allinson, who had taken her own life in 1945. Again, the première was entrusted to Pears and Britten.

During 1953, some of the opera was heard for the first time—the *Ritual Dances*, which Paul Sacher[8] had persuaded Tippett to organize into a concert suite. Sacher conducted the *Ritual Dances* in Basle in February that year. The opera itself was scheduled for the Royal Opera House, Covent Garden in 1955. Meanwhile, the Edinburgh Festival commissioned from Tippett a work to celebrate the tercentenary in 1953 of the birth of Corelli. The outcome was Tippett's *Fantasia Concertante on a Theme of Corelli*, for string orchestra. Sargent was due to conduct its first performance. Just beforehand he gave a press conference at which he spoke slightingly of the work: saying privately also that he intended 'to get the intellectuals out of music'. Tippett took over the première himself. Although it was neglected for some time afterwards, the Fantasia eventually became one of his best-known and best-loved works.

The climax of Tippett's education as a composer, and also the climax of the misunderstanding of his intentions, came with the first production of *The Midsummer Marriage* at Covent Garden in January 1955. Many fell in love with the music, though few grasped its dramatic import. The press made much of the alleged bafflement of the performers beforehand, even attributing to the singers expressions of disbelief which they had not uttered. The critics, led by Ernest Newman, dismissed it all as pretentious and obscure. To be fair, the composer had not made things easy for the producer (Christopher West), choreographer (John Cranko) and designer (Barbara Hepworth). He had specified too many of the details of the staging in his libretto. Also, the work was very long, and much of the dance music had to be cut. Tippett has learnt his lesson since then. Now he makes absolutely certain in advance that the formal proportions of his operas are right: and he gives only general indications to the producer and designer, entrusting the rest to their professional expertise.

The opera-going public and the critics were simply unprepared for a work that departed so far from the methods of Puccini and Verdi. Walton's *Troilus and Cressida*, first seen the previous year, was much more to their taste. Amongst those who did appreciate the masque-like character of Tippett's opera was Edward J. Dent. Otherwise, the 'magic' world of the temple and its inhabitants, the odd transformations of Mark and Jenifer, and the appearances of the mysterious Madame Sosostris left people baffled. Designer Barbara Hepworth had supplied an impressive neo-classic temple, but it was impractical. She imagined that the holes in the temple through which the lovers disappear would be apparent as a result of careful lighting. Unfortunately, the movement of the chorus in front of the temple interfered with this. Her abstract trees for Act II and the immobile temple itself took up badly needed stage space. The lighting of the temple at the very end of the opera was exciting, but it had little to do with the prescribed effect. In sum, the production took off in a somewhat different direction from that intended by the composer and, consequently, a lot of the audience found it clumsy and intractable. They blamed Tippett, of course. At best, *The Midsummer Marriage* was considered a brilliant failure: a failure exacerbated by the composer's own libretto, dubbed by one reviewer as 'one of the worst in the 350-year history of opera'.[9]

2 PREJUDICE AND REDISCOVERY

FOR A FEW YEARS it seemed likely that Tippett would forever be regarded merely as an inspired amateur. A whole succession of works after *The Midsummer Marriage* ran into trouble. A piano concerto, commissioned from Tippett by the City of Birmingham Symphony Orchestra, was declared unplayable by the original soloist, Julius Katchen. Fortunately, Louis Kentner was able and willing to step into the breach and the première took place as planned in 1956. Tippett had to transpose down a tone the whole of his Sonata for Four Horns (1955)—for otherwise the Dennis Brain Wind Ensemble deemed it impossible. Later performances by groups led by Alan Civil and Barry Tuckwell (who recorded the work) have restored it to its original pitch.

Worst of all, the first performance of Tippett's Second Symphony, at the Royal Festival Hall in February 1958, broke down after only a few pages. The conductor, Sir Adrian Boult, told the audience it was entirely his fault. A letter to *The Times* a few weeks later[10] implied that the composer was to blame. But the real culprit was the leader of the BBC Symphony Orchestra, Paul Beard. He had insisted on having the string parts re-barred in a conventional way, so that notes were not grouped across the bar-lines (as Tippett had written them, knowing how this would facilitate performance). Predictably, the new version seemed rhythmically incoherent to the players. Only later, when conductors like Colin Davis performed the work with the London Symphony Orchestra, and also recorded it with the same orchestra, was it clear that Tippett's original conception was both practical and lucid.

Tippett bore this all with cool, imperturbable good humour. He said later that if he survived it was only because he had 'the right mixture of patience and arrogance'. Soon the tide was to turn in his favour. A real coup, from which his reputation benefited enormously, was the production of his second opera, *King Priam*, at the Coventry Festival (arranged to celebrate the opening of the new cathedral there) in 1962. This had started life as a commission for a new choral work from the Koussevitsky Foundation, but had soon become an opera based on Homer. It had the advantage of a brilliant production by the film actor and director, Sam Wanamaker, with designs and lighting by Sean Kenny. There were the usual grumbles about the libretto which Tippett had written. Some critics, who had just discovered the magic of *The Midsummer Marriage*, lamented the change of musical style from lyricism to hard-hitting abrasiveness. But the competence of the composer was hardly called in question.

The turning-point in Tippett's fortunes came with a BBC studio performance of *The Midsummer Marriage* conducted by Norman Del Mar in 1963. Suddenly, everyone had discovered a forgotten operatic masterpiece and wanted a new production. Colin Davis heard the broadcast. A few years later he became Musical Director at Covent Garden: and in 1968 *The Midsummer Marriage* returned to the stage there in a new realization by Ande Anderson which, if it failed to tap the imaginative richness of the piece, proved it eminently stage-worthy. Davis himself conducted with unremitting inspiration. When his recording with the Covent Garden team was issued in 1971, it became a bestseller in Britain and the USA.

In 1965 Tippett reached the age of sixty. This helped his reputation no end. The accolades began to flow. Age had not withered him, nor custom staled his infinite variety. He was still young looking, still youthful in spirits, above all he was still composing. The amazement this caused was redoubled ten years later when he was seventy. Honours now arrived with greater frequency. Back in 1959, Tippett had been made a Commander of the British Empire. In 1966 he received a Knighthood; later, in 1979 he became a Companion of Honour. The Royal Academy and Royal College of Music had already made him an Honorary Fellow: but between 1964 and 1977 he received Honorary Doctorates from fourteen British Universities. In 1976 he was elected an Honorary Member of the American Academy of Arts and an Extraordinary Member of the Akademie der Kunste in Berlin. The same year he was awarded the Gold Medal of the Royal Philharmonic Society—an honour which he values above all others, since it came from his colleagues in the musical profession. In 1957, meanwhile, Tippett had been elected Chairman of the Peace Pledge Union and two years later became its President, a position he still holds. On account of his prison record, he remains debarred from jury service.

3   BRAVE NEW WORLDS

MANY COMPOSERS in their sixties and seventies slide gently into a mellow consolidation of past achievement. Tippett, if anything, began at this stage to live more dangerously. He was now quite fluent and more sure of himself. A pattern had appeared in his work whereby major dramatic compositions supplied potential ideas—formal and thematic—for several non-dramatic pieces. Thus, in the wake of *King Priam* came the Piano Sonata No. 2 (1962), Concerto for Orchestra (1963)—both of which received their premières at the Edinburgh Festival—and *The Vision of St. Augustine* (1963–65), a BBC commission: all of these pursued technical directions opened up by the opera. The conciseness of *King Priam* also paid great dividends in his later music.

Undoubtedly the real watershed in Tippett's life and work in the middle Sixties was his 'discovery' of America. He went there for the first time in 1965 as a guest composer at the music festival in Aspen, Colorado. Immediately, he fell in love with the canyons, mesas and deserts of Arizona, New Mexico and Utah. Later, he became equally excited about the big cities. In his youth, Tippett had been an inveterate hiker, exploring the English countryside, but since his Aspen visit he has returned many times to the States; and invitations to conduct and lecture have been a springboard for expeditions all over the American continent. The landscape and polyglot culture of America have filled his dreams and stimulated his imagination. Tippett has steeped himself in American literature and history;

33

he has found there a mixture of ideas and traditions analogous to the intellectual world of Shakespeare's England. He now almost regards the American scene as an extension of Shakespeare's culture into modern times.[11] Temperamentally, too, he has been attracted to America by the candour and openness which he encountered among the young people there. In sum, America became for him a 'newfound land of the spirit', and its influence is manifest in all his work since the late Sixties.

The first indications of American influence in Tippett's music comes in *The Shires Suite* (1965–70). This was written for the Leicestershire Schools Symphony Orchestra, with whom Tippett had recently become closely associated as guest conductor and artistic adviser. His programmes with the orchestra featured some American music—e.g. Copland's *Quiet City* and Ives's *Three Places in New England*; and there are many Ivesian passages in *The Shires Suite*. The ethos of America comes into the foreground in his next two operas, *The Knot Garden* (1966–70) and *The Ice Break* (1973–76); in the song-cycle, *Songs for Dov* (1970)—a kind of self-portrait embodied within a musician who goes imaginatively around the world journeying from innocence to experience—and in the vocal finale of the Third Symphony (1970–72).[12]

The love affair between Tippett and the USA has been mutual. Nowhere in the world has his music enjoyed so much success. With his visit there in 1974 to conduct the Chicago Symphony Orchestra in his Third Symphony and Piano Concerto, and to attend the American première of *The Knot Garden*—given by students at Northwestern University, Evanston, Illinois—Tippett began to reach the wider public in America. Students appeared at the Chicago concerts wearing tee-shirts with the slogan, 'Turn on to Tippett'. A few years later, in 1977, Georg Solti conducted the Chicago Symphony Orchestra in the Fourth Symphony—a Chicago Symphony commission, and the first major work by Tippett to receive its première outside England. Identifying completely with the piece, Solti took it to New York shortly afterwards, and insisted on including it in his European tour with the orchestra the

34

following year, when they played it at the Salzburg Festival and later made a recording of it. Soon after the Chicago première of the Fourth Symphony, Tippett shared the podium with Lorin Maazel in three concerts of his music with the Cleveland Orchestra. Mayor Perk proclaimed October 17–22 'Sir Michael Tippett-in-Cleveland Week': and the success of the occasion was reinforced by the appearance of the Prince of Wales, who prolonged his stay in the city to hear *A Child of Our Time*. During the week, the composer's advice on royal etiquette was continually solicited. While giving it, generously, he managed (on television) to remind his audience of his republican sympathies.

American appreciation of Tippett is symptomatic of the movement of his music generally out into the world at large. There are now Tippett fans in Hong Kong and Tokyo. The ubiquitous *A Child of Our Time* has found its way into several continents and cultures. The composer went to hear it performed in Zambia in 1975 by a (roughly 50–50) mixture of ex-patriate Europeans and native Zambians. In 1978, Tippett took his first extended break from composition in fifty years in order to go round the world, combining holidays with professional appearances. The impetus to do this came from the festivals at Perth and Adelaide in Australia, where Tippett's music was to be specially featured. In Adelaide, the first Australian production of a Tippett opera—*The Midsummer Marriage*—formed the opening event of the festival: and all performances of it sold out in advance. Tippett conducted his Fourth Symphony, and most of his songs and chamber music were also performed. On the way to Australia, he spent some time in Java and Bali, where the sounds of gamelan orchestras began to colour his ideas for his forthcoming Triple Concerto (1979). He returned via Hawaii and Los Angeles (where he conducted *A Child of Our Time*). Later the same year, Tippett revisited Aspen as guest composer and he also conducted at the Tanglewood Festival.

The spread of interest in Tippett's music has happened much more slowly in Europe than elsewhere. *A Child of Our Time*, it is true, has been performed many times on the continent.

Herbert von Karajan, no less, conducted it on one occasion in Italy, in 1952; against the composer's wishes, however, he had an interval half-way through Part II. Works like the Double Concerto and *Corelli Fantasia* found favour amongst such conductors as Hans Schmidt-Isserstedt. The composer himself conducted *The Vision of St. Augustine* (with the original soloist, Dietrich Fischer-Dieskau) at the Berlin Festival in 1966. But a production of *The Midsummer Marriage* in Karlsruhe (1973–74) was a failure; and when the same work was presented on French Radio (1978), with a cast and conductor (Richard Armstrong) drawn from Welsh National Opera, the Radio Orchestra misbehaved during rehearsals and as a result the second act had to be omitted.

Three reasons for this lack of response to Tippett's music on the continent come to mind. Firstly, in France and Italy, music is not as integral a feature of the educational system as it is in Britain and the USA. Thus there is no groundswell of informed opinion, coming from a younger generation of performers and listeners, comparable to that in the USA. Secondly, recordings of Tippett's music have also not been so generally available in these countries. Thirdly, in Germany and Austria, it is widely felt that the only contemporary music of quality belongs within the Viennese tradition. Many people there hardly acknowledge the existence of English music (Elgar—approved of by Strauss—Holst and Britten are striking exceptions). Only through the efforts of musicians based outside Europe has the later Tippett repertory penetrated these barriers. In the middle 1970s, Colin Davis and the London Symphony Orchestra wanted to take Tippett's Third Symphony to the Salzburg Festival: but Salzburg refused this work and Davis then refused to go. Georg Solti and the Chicago Symphony Orchestra were not, however, resisted and in 1978 brought the Fourth Symphony to Salzburg and Montreux before taking it to London. Later that year, Alexander Gibson and the Scottish National Orchestra took the same work to Warsaw and five other European cities; and the following year, Michael Rubenstein (conductor of the Illinois production of *The Knot Garden*) conducted a performance of the Third Symphony with the Vienna Symphony Orchestra. It should also be noted that the composer enjoyed some success in Stockholm and Helsinki, meanwhile, with concerts of his own music.

In the last fifteen years, Tippett has had to balance the increasing demands made upon him as a public figure against the privacy and isolation necessary for him to compose. He moved to a restored sixteenth-century house in Corsham, Wiltshire, living there for ten years (1960–70). Just before he moved yet again (1970) to an even more secluded house on the Marlborough Downs, he became Artistic Director of the Bath Festival, taking over from Yehudi Menuhin. Tippett helped rescue the festival from the brink of financial ruin. He broadened its scope and potential audience appeal. At his own insistence, he retained the position for only five years.

While in the Forties and Fifties he was a champion of the BBC Third Programme and gave many radio talks—some of these were published in a collection entitled *Moving Into Aquarius*, along with other reviews and essays, in 1959—in the Sixties and Seventies Tippett became increasingly drawn to television, again making a number of appearances himself, as well as becoming a keen follower of all kinds of TV entertainment (detective series, westerns, soap opera, etc.). The clichés of mass entertainment, along with the techniques employed by the media offered him important reference points, especially for his stage works, like *The Ice Break*.

In 1977, to coincide with the Covent Garden première of *The Ice Break*, Colin Davis brought together a group of Tippett's friends to organize a retrospective exhibition, *A Man of Our Time*, exemplifying Britain's appreciation and love for both the man and his achievements. Later, a travelling version of the exhibition was devised and has been seen all over the world.

Meanwhile, *The Ice Break* itself attracted full houses, partly because of the technologically advanced production designed by Ralph Koltai and produced by Sam Wanamaker, which involved the use of lasers. The following year, the Kiel Yachting Festival in Germany mounted a production of the opera similar in style to the Covent Garden one. In 1979, Sarah Caldwell produced and conducted the work in Boston—the first professional performance of a Tippett opera in the USA—and the work was the prime success of the season.

Since 1970, Tippett has suffered from poor eyesight. He now composes using large-size manuscript paper and reads with special magnifying glasses. Because of his eyesight, he has cut down on lecturing and conducting engagements. But the flow of composition remains unaffected. A heart irregularity diagnosed around 1970 is easily controlled by drugs: otherwise the composer remains remarkably healthy and full of energy. He revels in long walks through muddy fields and he engages in inter-continental travel and sight-seeing to a degree that would tax someone half his age. His only real problem is the psychosomatic stomach reaction which he suffers—often acutely—when subjected to excessive public exposure and uncritical adulation (which he detests). Doctors have probed and pondered, suggesting surgery as well as pills and medicine. But the only certain cure is still, apparently, marmalade: along with well planned holidays where Tippett can remain anonymous.

4 'TIS NATURE'S VOICE

WHEN MORLEY COLLEGE was hit by a landmine in 1940, Tippett found amid the rubble some library copies of the Purcell Society Edition. Studying these at leisure he was much stimulated by various formal procedures in Purcell's music— such as the ground bass and the fantasia. He also found some confirmation of aesthetic principles concerning relationships between words and music which T. S. Eliot had recently clarified for him, though to some extent he had known them previously in the context of Elizabethan madrigals. These principles now became quite fundamental to Tippett's work. We should, therefore, summarize them here.[13]

The arts all depend for their expressive power upon metaphor: a 'trick' whereby the inner world of the human psyche and the outer world are made suddenly to correspond, producing a memorable image of actuality. In the mixed art forms—ballet, drama and opera—the metaphorical component of *one* of the ingredients will always be dominant; indeed, it will swallow up the rest. In each of these art forms, a kind of hierarchy obtains: in ballet, gesture and movement are more important than music and plot; in drama, the words and plot take precedence over gesture and music; and in opera, music comes first, the words second, action and gesture, third. The result is invariably a unique fusion of elements carrying its own intrinsic power of metaphorical expression.

When words are set to music, the verbal metaphors are

'eaten up' by those within the music. It is almost unnecessary for the words to be heard individually; as long as the *situation* they express is embodied in the music, then all will be well. An 'inferior' text can be transformed by great music; conversely, an excellent piece of poetry will often be harmed by a musical setting, or will simply sabotage the musical operation which the composer has tried to perform upon it. The good operatic librettist is not someone who offers the composer a self-sufficient play to set to music. He must rather write words that will fit the composer's pre-established set of musical and dramatic porportions and his preconceived notions of what the music will be doing at any one stage. The same principle applies in an oratorio. It is also reflected in microcosm in songs, cantatas and other small-scale vocal forms.

Tippett's musical output includes a number of tiny experiments in word-setting. A pair of madrigals—settings of *The Windhover*, by Gerald Manley Hopkins, and *The Source*, by Edward Thomas, both dating from 1942—play with the extension of a single poetic image into a corresponding musical image. For another madrigal, *The Weeping Babe* (1944), Edith Sitwell wrote a special text which Tippett set line (or concept) by line, after the manner of the Elizabethan madrigalists. Tippett comments: 'I was intrigued by the way the poet softened sharp trochees, like "little" and "bitter" into gentle ones, like "flower" and "bower", and tried to see if I could extend the second syllable of the trochee by the melismata . . .' (Tippett once talked on this aspect of the madrigal before a performance. The poet, who was present, said afterwards, 'I shall never write a trochee again.') Another explicit piece of madrigal composition was *Dance, Clarion Air* written (in 1952) to a text 'tailor made' by Christopher Fry; Tippett's setting of Yeats's *Lullaby* (1960) also employs the same approach, even though the poem is strophic. Amongst Tippett's other short choral works are several settings of folk-songs; a *Magnificat and Nunc Dimittis* (1961); and a setting of the medieval Latin lyric, *Plebs Angelica* (1943), cast in the form of an antiphonal motet.

A crucial test of Tippett's skill in setting words to music came in the cantata, *Boyhood's End* (1943), where the text was an extract from W. H. Hudson's autobiography, *Far Away and Long Ago* (1918). Hudson's prose had to be organized and charged with musical poetry. The writer's backward glance at the crucial period of his boyhood's end, when he feared he might have lost his special gift of awareness of nature, had to be given an extra emotional intensity. Peter Pears[14] has pinpointed both the structural flexibility that enables this intensity to come about and also the skill with which Tippett causes the whole work to grow from the initial utterance— 'What, then, did I want?' The cantata is replete in subtle coloration of the words and uses Monteverdian or Purcellian vocal techniques of melismata for its most ardent expressive detail: words like 'uprising', 'dance', 'glist'ning', 'floating', and the final 'ecstasy' all achieve prominence in this fashion.

Tippett's flair for word-setting is an early feature of his coming to maturity as a composer. Around it there develops the easiest and most natural facet of his musical idiom. It can be observed later in the songs he wrote for an Old Vic Theatre production of Shakespeare's *The Tempest* in 1962—*Songs for Ariel*—and in those wherein he extends the character of Achilles outside the context of the opera *King Priam*—*Songs for Achilles* (1961). The first of the Achilles songs appears in the second act of the opera itself, showing the Greek hero sulking in his tent and singing nostalgically to his friend, Patroclus. The other two songs (independent of the opera) also relate to Patroclus, live and dead. The second comes to a climax in each of its three stanzas on Achilles' war-cry, *Oi-o* (A Greek cry of aggression). In the third, Achilles—after the shock of Patroclus' death— invokes his divine mother, Thetis. She appears out of the sea, and after Achilles has spoken, sinks back again into her immortality, to the same guitar music as before, heard in reverse. Tippett's vocal line here cleverly encompasses both roles in a fluid declamatory recitative.

Tippett's early absorption with word-setting results in a vocal quality within most of his thematic invention: cf. ex. 1,

an oboe melody from the first Ritual Dance in *The Midsummer Marriage*. In a sense, all Tippett's finest musical ideas are singable; conversely, it should be remembered that as he composes at the piano, he sings everything, simply to test it out. Also, working upon songs and choral pieces—amongst them, numerous folk-song arrangements and a children's cantata, *Crown of the Year*—provided him with an apt context within which to develop those facets of his expression which needed to be explored in oratorios and stage works.

Tippett, in his mid-thirties, discovered himself to be essentially a two-sided creator: one who emulated Beethoven as the purveyor of humanist messages to mankind; and one who followed Stravinsky as an ardent exponent of music with an independent life of its own, with intrinsic formal and expressive potential. Tippett's first mature attempt at a work with a message was his oratorio, *A Child of Our Time*.

5 DEATH'S REPUBLIC

TIPPETT BEGAN WRITING the music for *A Child of Our Time* a few days after the outbreak of war in 1939. Fearing that he might be wiped out in an air-raid, he wrote it at great speed. The long gestation period for the work had cost him a lot of effort. But eventually, he became clear as to his aims and intentions, and carried the composition through to its final stages with some facility.

Examining Tippett's *Sketch for a Modern Oratorio*[15]—the title he gave the draft scenario which he took to T. S. Eliot when he was hoping the poet would provide him with a text—we can see that certain key decisions regarding the shape and content of the work underlie its success. Firstly, the choice of oratorio rather than operatic format ensured that there would be an overriding emphasis on *reflection*. The incidents that provoked the piece are absorbed into a larger framework wherein the actions and reactions of men in general can be considered. At virtually every stage we step back from events and regard them in a wider context. Whereas the focal point of Handel's oratorios and Bach's Passions is always a named individual, the 'child of our time' here is nameless, though no less significant. As with the Unknown Soldier, we know who and what the 'child' represents—the eternal scapegoat, a figure present in all periods and in all societies. The title of Tippett's oratorio is taken from a novel, *Ein Kind unserer Zeit* (1938), by the prominent anti-Nazi writer and dramatist Ödön von Horvath

43

(1902–38). But this in no way ties the piece to a place or period. Occasionally, Tippett's response to the immediate political situation comes to the surface, e.g. in the Spiritual of Anger, 'Go down Moses'. The Chorus of the Self-Righteous, 'We cannot have them in our Empire' could represent equally the attitudes of American WASPS, the British National Front, Amin's Ugandan government or the German Nazis of the 1930s. Generally, however, Tippett is concerned with matters more fundamental and timeless. Any appreciation of the work must, therefore, base itself on respect for its anonymity.

Modelling the oratorio on Handel's *Messiah*, Tippett uses a tripartite scheme in which 'Part I deals with the general state of oppression in our time; Part II presents the particular story of a young man's attempt to seek justice by violence and the catastrophic consequences; while Part III considers the moral to be drawn, if any.'[16] Tippett also adopts devices common to the Handelian oratorio and Bach Passions: recitative for narration; choral description; contemplative arias; and the congregational hymn. He explicitly evokes *Messiah* in the Chorus of the Oppressed (No. 5)—cf. Handel's 'He trusted in God that He would deliver him'—and in the opening chorus of Part II, comparable to 'Behold the Lamb of God' at the start of Part II of Handel's oratorio (ex. 2).

Handel: *Messiah*

The homage to Bach is overt in some of the choruses of Part II: 'Let Him be crucified' from the *St. Matthew Passion*, for instance, is mirrored in Tippett's 'Away with them! Curse them! Kill them!' (No. 11); and this same Double Chorus of Persecutors and Persecuted owes its questioning 'Where? Why? How?' to Bach's opening double-chorus in the same work. Again, Tippett's Chorus of the Self-Righteous echoes 'We have a law' in Bach's *St. John Passion*. Nevertheless, we are here manifestly dealing with something other than the feeble imitations of baroque oratorio and Passion that proliferated in England especially during the Victorian period. Tippett always renews and revitalizes his original models.

The chief mode of renewal is that of irony. To give a straightforward example, the Jewish villains of Bach's 'We have a law', mentioned above, are here the *victims* in Tippett's equivalent chorus. But most crucial in giving a new and ironic slant to the traditional oratorio format was the choice of Negro spirituals for the congregational hymns. Originally, it seemed an odd decision; and even Eliot asked Tippett if the chorus would have to 'black up' for these. The composer's view was that all races everywhere could identify with the sentiments of Negro spirituals. The corresponding appeal of Lutheran chorales or Jewish melodies would be more limited.

Tippett observed that the spirituals themselves 'have turned and twisted Bible language into a modern dialect: the stories they tell of Bible Jews are used to comfort Negroes in the bitterness of oppression.' They could thus be used to symbolize 'the agony of modern Jews in Hitler's Europe' along with any who are 'rejected, cast out from the centre of our society onto the. fringes: into slums, into concentration camps, into ghettoes.'[17]

Tippett first heard spirituals in a radio broadcast in 1938, when his planning of the oratorio was already under way. The singing, he recalls, was very bad. But when (in 'Steal away') it reached the phrase, 'The trumpet sounds within-a my Soul', he was 'shot through with the sudden realization that the melody was far greater than the individual singer and had the power to move us all.' He then obtained from America a volume of spirituals and five of these he incorporated into his *Sketch* for Eliot.[18] Outlining for Eliot a suggested basis for the text for the rest of the oratorio (on the right-hand pages of the *Sketch*), he tried to match the 'lapidaric' verbal style of the spirituals deriving from folk-idioms. Sometimes he succeeded, as in the line 'Let them starve in No-Man's Land'; occasionally, he spoilt the effect by allowing some more sophisticated psychological jargon to obtrude, as in 'I am caught between my desires and their frustration as between the hammer and the anvil'. In spite of such flaws, the text and music for *A Child of Our Time* marry together into a telling and powerful utterance simply because of their closeness throughout to the vernacular.

The general musical style of the piece was also affected by the presence of the spirituals. The composer comments thus: 'I used the interval of a minor third, produced so characteristically in the melodies of the spirituals when moving from the fifth of the tonic to the flat seventh, as a basic interval of the whole work—sometimes on its own, sometimes superimposed upon the open fifth below the whole note. These intervals (minor third, fifth and flat seventh) could lead on the one hand to a kind of sliding chromatic fugue (cf. No. 5, Chorus of the Oppressed); and on the other to a Weill-like tango (cf. No. 6, the tenor solo, "I have no money for my bread"); or even to a dance-like accompaniment (cf. No. 27, the alto solo, "The soul of man").'[18]

At the same time, Tippett 'improved' the spirituals, rejecting most of the harmonizations in the volume from which he had taken them, and clarifying their linear texture. Moreover, he found his own way of dramatizing them by pitting the soloists against the chorus. In this he took his cue from the singing of the Hall Johnson Choir, which he had heard on the soundtrack to the film *Green Pastures* (Warner Bros., 1936).

When Tippett produced his *Sketch* for Eliot, the latter considered it for some weeks and then 'gave me the surprising advice to write all the words myself. He felt the *Sketch* was already a text in embryo (as, in fact, it was) and whatever words, he, Eliot, wrote would be of such greater poetic quality they would "stick out a mile".'[19]

Tippett took his advice, and in doing so, came to realize for himself the basic working principle that was thenceforth to be the foundation of all his major compositions. In Tippett's later works, as in *A Child of Our Time*, the composer's inner feelings are given objective substance in a musical scheme which swallows up, in the process, a lot of dramatic and philosophical material—ideas and images drawn from a variety of sources. But in the final fusion it is always the music that is dominant.

A superficial glance through the *Sketch* for Tippett's oratorio shows the composer piecing together the work from disparate experiences—personal, literary, visual and musical. Overall, however, within the three parts of the oratorio, there is a pattern of movement that takes us from the general to the particular and back again. The soloists are only specifically identified as the Boy, Mother etc. in Part II. The opening chorus and alto solo give us a view of the world, as if from another planet, after the manner of the Prologue in Heaven from Goethe's *Faust*—and the succeeding chorus (mankind in general) identifies with this. Tippett makes use of the seasonal metaphor here, depicting the 'winter of the world' (after Wilfred Owen's poem, *The Seed*) which only becomes spring at the end of the work.

We meet the main theme of the oratorio in the succeeding tenor solo (No. 6): the psychologically divided Man, at odds with his Shadow. To turn the personal agonies inherent in this theme into a sufficiently generalized form caused the composer a lot of trouble. This is evident from the notes he provided for Eliot in the *Sketch*, couched in Jungian language: 'The man tells of his psychological split self which appears to him and actually is on a certain plane the frustrations of his condition in the commonwealth. He has lost the relation to his soul, to the impersonal things, hence the feminine, the women have demonic power (or he has an infantile fixation etc.). He projects the *anima* on his women-folk with devastating personal misunderstandings and complexes.' When Tippett finalized the text for this aria, he omitted from his suggested original the lines 'Women have hold on my entrails, how can I grow to a man's stature': the end-result is less private and personal.[20]

The healing of the rift with which he is preoccupied comes only in the final General Ensemble (No. 29), where it is clearly and movingly encapsulated: 'I would know my Shadow and my light/so shall I at last be whole.' This is pre-figured in the alto solo 'The soul of man' (No. 27) which is jointly inspired by Jung and by one of Blake's illustrations to the *Book of Job*—'. . . when Job reaches the point at which he cannot distinguish the action of God from the action of Satan, the Divine Mercy shows him the mystery of re-birth into a new synthesis.' On the Boy's final affirmation, 'I would know my shadow and my light', Tippett has commented more recently, '[This sentence] is very easy to say, very difficult to do. I hold it to be just possible for individuals, but impossible for collectives in our present climate of self-righteousness—of groups,

The composer on holiday in Spain
with Wilfred Franks, *circa* 1932

Michael Tippett (right) aged about
seven, with his brother Peter

Tippett in Zambia in 1975

Michael Tippett conducting the Leicestershire Schools Symphony Orchestra in the late Sixties

Tippett conducting the English Chamber Orchestra in a Queen Elizabeth Hall rehearsal on 9 January 1980

societies, nations.'[21]

Without doubt, *A Child of Our Time* galvanized all Tippett's creative energies, resulting in a work that was a watershed in his development: for it contains far more ideas and possibilities than he could ever exploit in a single composition. In his output as a whole, it is also unique on account of its sustained directness of expression and almost limpid simplicity (qualities he tried to emulate from Berlioz' *L'Enfance du Christ*, which he heard on the radio at that time). But such restraint is deceptive. On close acquaintance, the oratorio reveals features that are distinctive to the composer.

Tippett's consistently linear approach to choral and orchestral writing is absent entirely in the music of his contemporaries. This is the fruit of Tippett's interest in Renaissance music. Right from the opening orchestral introduction, the tensions of madrigalian counterpoint are prevalent: other examples are the short linking interludes in Nos. 2 and 3 and the Praeludium before No. 29.

Tippett has always heard as one and the same thing the blues inflexions of jazz and the expressive chromaticism of Wilbye, Monteverdi and Purcell. He is thus able to produce a fusion of the two in—to take but one poignant example—the soprano solo, 'How can I cherish my man' where the unity of the work is not demonstrable only in terms of thematic relationships. It is born of the consistency of Tippett's language. Clearly, too, Tippett became more assured in his deployment of that language as his work on the oratorio proceeded. In Part III, he achieves a fine synthesis of techniques and imagery to match the attainment of 'wholeness' in his subject matter. The very opening chorus, 'The cold deepens' introduces that mode of nature-based archetypal experience which is a portent of what Tippett has in store in his later compositions.

A Child of Our Time established a pattern in Tippett's work whereby he would never attempt an immediate creative response to tragic incident. He has always detached himself, recollecting the tragic emotion in tranquillity, and the work emerges embodying a wider perspective. An outstanding example of this is Tippett's song-cycle, *The Heart's Assurance*. Francesca Allinson—to whose memory it is dedicated—took her life under the strain not just of personal heartbreak but of the war which was only now ending. Tippett, in commemorating her, selected poems by two young writers who died in the war, Alun Lewis and Sidney Keyes. From these he fashioned a sequence with the general theme, 'Love under the shadow of death' (which nearly became a subtitle). True to his aesthetic, Tippett obliterates the distinctions between the two poets in setting their verse to music. As he points out, 'The "music" of the verse merely provided me with raw material for my own music.'[22] He thus makes a special expressive highlighting of the 'he's' and 'she's' in the third song, *Compassion*, shaping and colouring them in the same way with long, expressive notes: this occurs all the time in the original poetry. Like Schubert adding the secondary image of the spinning-wheel to his setting of Goethe's *Gretchen am Spinnrade*, so Tippett adds a contextual image of distance in his treatment of the last song, *Remember your Lovers*, so that we can 'imagine a young woman singing out over the Elysian fields to the young man in the fields beyond'.

Throughout the cycle, love and death are polarized within the verbal and musical imagery. The contrast becomes most explicit in the last song. Here each stanza begins with a sort of vocalized reminiscence of the Last Post, declaimed unaccompanied and answered each time with a subdued fanfare-with-drums motif in the piano part though this military motif on the piano is soon lost in the swirling lyrical decorations that typify the song. At its fourth and final appearance, the refrain is *accompanied by* the military motif and the arresting perfect fifth interval of the Last Post is raised eloquently by a semitone.

Since *The Heart's Assurance* is a product of the same compositional phase as *The Midsummer Marriage*, it is not surprising that love and lyricism here overwhelm death and rhetoric. Love is quite plainly portrayed as a stronger force than aggression or extinction. The first, third and fourth songs almost suppress any hints of conflict. The first remembers the innocence of seduction and the vocal line is swathed in pianistic caresses. The third builds its rhetoric from images of compassionate love. The fourth, almost a sketch for the third Ritual Dance in *The Midsummer Marriage*, conjures the gaiety of love defiant in the context of death. Throughout these songs there seems to be no deliberate check on Tippett's free-wheeling lyricism with its characteristic tonal elisions. The art in the work is prodigious but concealed.

Each of the strophes in the first song undergoes pointed transformations, some incidental, some fundamental. The vocal addresses to the journeyman, the soldier and the lonely wife are the same for the first two, then modified for the third: a seventh on the subdominant of B minor becomes a *gentler* seventh on the leading note of F major. The gentle pianistic throbbing that underpins the last four words of 'Before this endless belt began its cruel revolution' is used as a modulatory device at 'things turned bad'; and its point is made explicit at 'Before your lover left this life'. The same kind of insistence— whereby the lyrical flow of the music is retarded by a pedal-point—comes in the motif for 'Death taps down every street' in the coda to the song. Thus, the presence of symbolic disturbances to the lyrical abundance of the work gives it its strength and toughness. *The Heart's Assurance* delineates human love, passion and heartbreak with a depth and directness only an artist in his prime might accomplish. Small wonder that at this stage Tippett felt fit and able to tackle the larger canvas of opera.

6 ILLUSION AND ACTUALITY

TIPPETT'S OPERAS constitute a genre in their own right. They are quite distinct from those of his British contemporaries and even, possibly, from those of most of his European or American counterparts. With many of them, symbolism is an optional extra, an ingredient that may or may not help deepen an experience of stage actuality. Sometimes it is an interference. With Tippett's operas, symbolism is of the essence. Tippett's tendency in his oratorio to distance himself from the commonplace is extensively developed in his stage works. Tippett uses the stage—the singers, the orchestra, elements of presentation—more like an innovatory playwright. He is far removed from the opera composers, especially the nineteenth-century Italians, who asked themselves first and foremost, 'Who shall I have singing in the next opera?' or questions of the same order. Tippett instead goes back to older traditions and the stage for him has a magical aura. His plots are concerned with what Jean Cocteau (writing about his dramatic and film treatments of the Orpheus Legend) calls 'frontier incidents'. Thus his characters move freely backwards and forwards between their actual selves and their mythological and other prototypes. Such a method might easily have been a recipe for disaster; but fortunately, when he came to write his major works for the stage, Tippett knew largely what he was after. Even with his first opera, *The Midsummer Marriage*, the spell works much more powerfully than anyone at first imagined.

The Midsummer Marriage begins where *A Child of Our Time* leaves off. Its point of departure is the final prayer for renewal and regeneration in the oratorio—'I would know my shadow and my light'. Like the earlier work, it draws upon a wealth of accumulated skills, invention and experience. During Tippett's early years, he had experimented, in four (unpublished) pieces, with different dramatic genres: *The Village Opera* (1929) and *Robin Hood* (1934) are both ballad operas; *Robert of Sicily* (1938) is a children's opera to a text by Christopher Fry; *Seven at a Stroke* (1939) is a play by Fry with music arranged by Tippett. But the composer was quite certain then that a full scale opera for professional performance was something he should only write when he was ready for it, and when it could be allowed its proper period of gestation.

The outcome, when he eventually wrote *The Midsummer Marriage*, as with *A Child of Our Time*, was comparable to Stravinsky's experience in writing *Le Sacre du Printemps*: for in relation to these works, Tippett too could say, 'I am the vessel through which [they] passed . . .' Both are compositions that welled up inside him, took over his whole existence and demanded objectification in some concrete form outside himself. Thus, later, he was able to declare: 'I hold for myself that the composition of oratorio and opera is a collective as well as a personal experience. While indeed all artistic creation may be seen in that way, I believe the collective experience, whether conscious or unconscious, is more fundamental to an oratorio or an opera than to a string quartet.' [23]

Essentially, *The Midsummer Marriage* is about one human relationship viewed from different angles. To realize this technically, Tippett had to stir new life into an art form which all too readily became encrusted with routine modes and formulae. As in operas of the past, we can find here arias, duets, ensembles and chorus episodes. But *The Midsummer Marriage* places a new emphasis upon the symbolic power of stage illusion. This is clear from the fact that the main working out of the drama (in Act II) and the climax and dénouement (Act III) are articulated through ballet: the famous sequence of *Ritual Dances* (published and often performed as an independent concert item) which—even in the 1950s, when the opera as a whole was regarded as a failure—many esteemed highly.

Tippett's aim in the opera is to communicate a vision of wholeness, an integrity of mind, heart and body. He does this through a modern version of the traditional plot about the unexpected hindrances to an eventual marriage. The old hindrances—social ones—are no longer relevant. They belong to a past age and to past dramatic tradition. The marriage of king and commoner (to take an extreme example) is rarely now a matter of violent controversy—certainly not to the extent it was in 1938, for instance, when King Edward VIII had to abdicate from the British throne in order to marry Mrs Simpson. Now, in present day society, the real hindrance is 'our ignorance or illusion about ourselves'.

The plot of the opera is fairly easily assimilated, once one has come to terms with the initial stage metaphor which Tippett employs for the falling apart of the two lovers, Mark and Jenifer, when, in Act I, they meet on their wedding-day. Here, Tippett has tried to project directly in dramatic terms something from his own imagination, a moment of sudden illumination in which he saw 'a stage picture (as opposed to hearing a musical sound) of a wooded hilltop with a temple, where a warm and soft young man was being rebuffed by a cold and hard young woman . . . to such a degree that the collective, magical archetypes take charge—that Jung's *anima* and *animus*—the girl, inflated by the latter, rises through the stage-flies to heaven, and the man, overwhelmed by the former, descends through the stage-floor to hell. But it was clear they would soon return. For I saw the girl later descending in a costume reminiscent of the goddess Athena . . . and the man ascending in one reminiscent of the god Dionysus . . .'[24]

All this is integrated into the action of Act I. The chorus waiting to celebrate the runaway marriage of Mark and Jenifer are frightened off by some strange people who appear from a temple at sunrise. Mark, too, argues with the Temple inhabitants, then quarrels with Jenifer, whereupon they go off in different directions. King Fisher tries to trace Jenifer without

54

success; at the climax of his frustration Mark and Jenifer return strangely transformed: and, becoming even more at logger-heads, they disappear off again.

Even from such a bald summary of the events of Act I, and without following the plot further, it is evident that Tippett's conception of opera is poles apart from that favoured by his contemporaries, such as Britten, Walton, Bliss or Berkeley, all of whom have worked within the tradition of Verdi and Puccini. With all of the latter, one can expect a straight-forward story-line and characterization manifestly close to everyday life. Considered especially from a *verismo* standpoint, Mark and Jenifer may seem particularly 'un-real'. Their transformations are certainly not everyday occurrences—other than in the extreme psychological manifestations we tend to label 'schizophrenic'; but it is precisely their psychology that Tippett brings alive in his music. Meanwhile, he complements them with a pair of (so to speak) earthbound lovers: Bella (who is secretary to Jenifer's father, King Fisher) and her boyfriend, a mechanic called Jack. The chorus, to complete the picture, is made up of their friends of both sexes.

While Tippett puts *verismo* presentation on one side, he does recognize many other theatrical modes. In fact, *The Midsummer Marriage* is an amalgam of related dramatic traditions. Like *The Magic Flute*, it is a quest opera: its central hero and heroine are engaged in a search for illumination. The task of the music then becomes to help us 'suspend the critical and analytical judgement, without which happening no experience of the numinous can be immediate at all'.[25] Linked to this is the masque, and the magical world of Shakespeare's *A Midsummer Night's Dream*. 'Part of my entertainment,' the composer writes, 'is the interaction of two worlds, though the supernatural world I conjure is not a fairy world but another.'[26]

As with the Statue in *Don Giovanni*, or Bottom when he acquires an ass's head, so, too, with the principal lovers in *The Midsummer Marriage*: they also are able to enter 'a different range of experience from anyone else'. That 'other' world is represented by a temple 'peopled by a wise priest and priestess [He-Ancient and She-Ancient], to whom I gave a chorus of

55

neophytes in the shape of a group of dancers who are silent'.[27]

The names of the characters themselves have important resonances bearing upon this differentiation of two 'worlds' within the opera: royal Cornish names for the 'marvellous' couple, Mark and Jenifer; functional names for Jack and Bella; King Fisher is up-to-date American (like Duke Ellington) but also the impotent Fisher King of Jessie L. Weston's *From Ritual to Romance*; Madame Sosostris is the fortune-teller in Weston's book (the latter two both used also by T. S. Eliot in *The Waste Land*).

Classical precedent also shapes the opera. For each main scene can be considered an *agon*, or dramatic contest, after the manner of Aristophanes. It is thus that our interest is held, especially in the extended outer acts. The main exception here is the long monologue for Madame Sosostris in Act III, in which the composer takes us for a moment outside the action of the opera, and relives the agonies of artistic creation in music of unforgettable power, anguish and eventual serenity. This is the turning-point of Act III—for it sets in motion the struggle between the actual and supernatural worlds, between 'the old father and the whole young world, with the hero and heroine united'. It is nevertheless the most difficult scene to present visually with absolute conviction.

Tippett has always felt that opera—to survive and remain a vital force—must relate to the contemporary theatre. In his own work, this meant at first a relationship with the verse-drama of Auden, Eliot and Christopher Fry: and this survives in the background to his later operas, even when Brechtian techniques or those of television and the cinema seem to have taken over. Here, in *The Midsummer Marriage*, Tippett links the tradition of *A Midsummer Night's Dream* with the theatrical world of Eliot 'whose stage is generally a stage of "depth"—by which I mean that we sense, especially at certain designed moments, another world within or behind the world of the stage set'. Moreover, as in *The Family Reunion*, the characters in Tippett's opera only become aware of their real selves in the course of the plot.

The uniqueness of Tippett's score lies precisely in its ability

to articulate the contrasts between the actual and the supernatural in the opera. We meet this in the opening scene of Act
I. After the exuberant music that brings on the chorus,
everything becomes gradually still and a celesta motif,
answered by flutes and accompanied by a single note *tremolo* on
the violas, signifies the appearances of the mysterious temple
(ex. 3): immediately, our disbelief is suspended and we are

ready to go 'within or behind the world of the stage set'. A little
march marks the entrance of the dancers and ancients (ex. 4).

This establishes the contrast between the hieratic and the
lyrical, which is the musical basis of the *agon* in this scene and
which is developed throughout the opera. In such a contrast we
can see the germ of that mosaic technique which takes over
completely the musical presentation of all the ingredients in
Tippett's subsequent operas. It arises from the sharply defined

57

brilliance of his orchestration, and from the Purcellian dramatic vocalization of the words which he uses to enhance the impact of the characters.

Mark—whom we first encounter singing a rapturous hymn to the ascending lark on midsummer morning, in wonderfully ornate vocal lines—is shown on the same declamatory level as Jenifer at their initial meeting. When they return, later in Act I, from their respective 'other' worlds, they are sharply distinguished. She is like St. Joan (according to Tippett's sketches), her soul wafting high within some visionary trance.[28] He remains hotly passionate, fiercely Dionysian. Her aria, baroque and hieratic in style, with trumpet obbligato, identifies her with the temple inhabitants and their world: for this very reason, the aria should always be choreographed. His proud rhetoric, accompanied by a Verdi-like thrumming on strings, supported by woodwind, draws him even closer to the young folk around him. When the two of them reappear in Act III, now reconciled, the distinctions between the different strata in the music have been swept away.

We have a clue in the libretto as to what has happened. 'She must leap and he must fall,' sing the chorus before the Ritual Dances—but later the personal pronouns are reversed. Thus Mark and Jenifer have passed through the two gates of mutual understanding, the high and the low, eventually returning in the glory of a symbolic union. And when, at the end, we realize that the wheel has come full circle, and that we are at the dawn of another day, the music can return to the ecstatic lyricism of the very opening scenes. A quotation in the libretto from W. B. Yeats encapsulates the new-found hope and regenerative impulse:

> All things fall and are built again
> And those that build them again are gay.[29]

Tippett's vision of wholeness and integrity is complete.

Tippett is no less convincing or sensitive in his treatment of the more conventional lovers, Jack and Bella. Their dreams of marriage and domestic bliss are not at all incongruous. Indeed, to have them in the opera strengthens our awareness that, for all its illusionistic and other-worldly qualities, the opera connects with the known world outside the opera house.

Many of Tippett's operatic characters are composite figures, pieced together from a variety of individuals, real and mythological, and stereotypes from the past and present. Sometimes the constituent elements are not cemented strongly enough to form a personality that is totally credible. This is true of King Fisher, here. A Shavian villain and a staunchly Victorian father, we understand him as a representative of the older generation, of an older society whose values were based on the accumulation of wealth and family stability. King Fisher registers in Act I mainly in generalized terms, for he communicates primarily through his secretary Bella. The subtler details of his character also tend to be swept away in a flood of excitable music. On the other hand, his confrontation with the Ancients in Act III and subsequent death are moving, not because he was a real villain, or even an unsympathetic character, but because destiny has overtaken him. His death is necessary for a fresh burgeoning of life to occur. At this point, we realize that King Fisher carries deeper mythological resonances—e.g. he might be the King of Egypt who, in the traditional mummers' play, is slain by St. George and brought to life again—but this is all too late for an operatic audience forming a conception of his character. King Fisher gave Tippett some trouble as the abundance of sketches relating to this character show.

Even more than in *A Child of Our Time*, nature metaphors are part of the action in *The Midsummer Marriage*. They belong to, and articulate for us, the other world 'within or behind the world of the stage set'. We are shown the passing of the hours on midsummer's day—from dawn to midday, in Act I, through the heat of the afternoon, in Act II, to starry night and the chilly mist-enveloped dawn with which the opera ends. Nature takes over, symbolically, in the Ritual Dances of Acts II and III.[30] The action in three of them involves the pursuit of a male by a female: the hound chases the hare; the otter hunts the fish; the hawk hunts the bird—all female predators aiming to

59

cause the death of the male. When the hawk strikes down the bird, Bella, watching it 'with increasing fascination and horror ... not knowing if what she sees is real or her own dreams', screams and interrupts the dance. The final dance—Fire in Summer—is only possible when King Fisher has died and a transfiguration can occur which brings back Mark and Jenifer reconciled and united.

The musical essence of the opera is contained in these dances. They exemplify its use of diatonic harmony, extended, indeed rejuvenated, by the persistence of superimposed fourths. The interval of the descending fourth becomes a kind of leitmotiv effect throughout the work: just before the climax of the final Ritual Dance, this is crystallized in a melodic sequence of descending fourths, stretching from high trumpet to bass trombone (ex. 5).

The music of *The Midsummer Marriage* seems ever to expand outwards, yet is always returning inwards. This concentric formal feature is again aptly exemplified in the Ritual Dances. Tippett acquired from Purcell an immense fondness for ground-bass forms: these feature particularly in the first two Ritual Dances, but never more movingly than at the death of King Fisher, when his body is carried out, the chorus, He-Ancient and She-Ancient reflecting on his fate. Above all, the opera deposits a memory of superabundant high-flown invention always of a high order. It is a long work, but its proportions are well thought out. Originally it was going to be a two-act opera, with the dances as an interlude. Fortunately, Tippett was persuaded to expand the design into a three-act presentation.[31] The resultant scheme was a perfect vehicle for his teeming store of invention.

In Act III of *The Midsummer Marriage*, when Mark and Jenifer attain the illumination for which they have searched, the He-Ancient (in the final Ritual Dance) sings:

> *Fate and Freedom are a paradox,*
> *Choose the fate but yet the God*
> *Speaks through whatever fate we choose.*

This is Tippett's point of departure for his next opera, *King Priam*, and indeed his two subsequent operas. *King Priam* is a tragedy, in the Racinian sense of dealing with unavoidable destiny. Tippett had become convinced that the notion of tragedy was creatively feasible in the modern epoch, partly as a result of seeing Jean-Louis Barrault company's production of the Claudel/Milhaud *Christophe Colombe* in London in 1956, partly, also, through reading a book on Racine (and Pascal) by Lucien Goldmann, *Le Dieu Caché*.[32] *King Priam* thus shows us the 'absolute solitude of the tragic characters under the gaze of the hidden God'—the 'hidden God' being, of course, fate or destiny.[33]

Its plot is extracted from Homer but its theme is 'the

mysterious nature of human choice', seen in the relations between Priam, King of Troy, Hecuba his wife, his sons, Hector and Paris, and their wives, Andromache and Helen.[34] Whereas in Homer, war is in the foreground, here it is only a backcloth to the main action. Our attention is focused upon the six protagonists, three male, three female. Their lives and relations with each other affected by the circumstances of war, they are primarily preoccupied with a series of choices, each one entailing the need to distinguish personal desire and fulfilment from social and political duty.

To attain the right kind of presentation, Tippett emulates Brecht and the Shakespeare history plays, organizing his epic material into a sequence of scenes and commentaries. The libretto becomes a scheme of situations, concisely expressed, pared away until it is just a bone-structure to be fleshed out with music. The pace is fast. Dramatic monologues predominate, enabling the characters to reflect upon the choices with which they are faced, upon destiny, and upon the meaning of human existence. The vocal style of the opera is mainly declamatory; lyricism is subordinate. Paris and Helen, for example, are not allowed a love duet in which to unburden their passion. Instead Paris is made to consider the catastrophic consequences of his abduction of Helen in a self-questioning monologue. In the course of the opera, the characters rarely establish relationships: they tend only to interact. This is to the point. Fate is invincible; humankind is its instrument. Tippett's music mirrors the interlocking of the two.

King Priam is unusual in Tippett's operatic *oeuvre*. In addition to being based on given story material—rather than on something invented anew by the composer—its characters are drawn directly from Homer. They are not modified, moulded or merged with any other theatrical, historical or mythological figures outside the Homeric world. Tippett's sole ploy of that sort—and it is a brilliant ploy—is to join together the three female protagonists and the three goddesses, to one of whom Paris is invited to give the apple in the final scene of Act I. For Paris, the goddesses Athene, Hera and Aphrodite are models of the three women in his life—Hecuba, Andromache and Helen, respectively—so Tippett arranges for the roles to be taken by the same three singers. Paris, of course, opts for Aphrodite, simultaneously choosing Helen in the process.

The opera contains no other reinforcement of the characters, no further outside connections or internal correspondences. Music alone underlines the stage action and characterization. *King Priam* is not a documentary presentation of historical events. It highlights the factors which are contingent to the Homeric epic—factors none the less important because they survive in every generation up to the present. They are the eternal problems of the human heart and of human destiny. In Tippett's words, the opera is concerned with 'the values that arise from the Past staged with an intense sense of the Present'.

Of necessity, Tippett altered his musical style and formal procedures to serve his freshly defined theatrical aims. In *The Midsummer Marriage*, the voices 'ride on a roughly homogeneous flow of orchestral sound'.[35] Here, in *King Priam*, we find a mosaic of instrumental gestures relating to all the ingredients and personalities in the drama. Debussy's caricature of Wagner's *leitmotiv* method, whereby each character presents his musical visiting-card when appearing on stage, is possibly more apposite in the case of *King Priam*. Nevertheless, things are not that simple. The mosaic that unfolds here embodies all the metaphors through which Tippett can re-evoke 'the values that arise from the Past' and re-charge them with meaning.

Their articulation entails a radical re-thinking of the opera orchestra, its function and format. Hearing the first British performance of Stravinsky's *Agon* (1957), conducted by Tippett's friend, John Minchinton, provided him with a strong impetus to undertake such a reorganization. The barest minimum of music is allied to the most economical use of the orchestra. Sometimes only a single instrument or a tiny group of instruments play. The cry of the child Paris in Scene I is given to an oboe. The cradling of the child is done by bass triplets on the harp. Priam's regal strength is expressed by two horns set between high and low piano octaves. The Wise Old Man who comes to interpret Hecuba's dream is allotted murky music for bass-clarinet, bassoon and contrabassoon. Only when the dream has been interpreted—presaging Priam's death at the hands of his son, Paris—and Hecuba and Priam have to choose between killing the child or immediately accepting Fate by letting him live, only then do the strings enter. Hecuba's response—'Then am I no longer mother to this child'—is declaimed against fast figurations on violins (which are not divided into first and second groups as is usual). Priam's anguish, his sense of divided loyalties—'A father and a king'—is expressed over violas, cellos and basses, *divisi*. Although the orchestration is spare, Tippett's invention tells. The listener adjusts to its processes quickly. He is likely to be unaware, unless told in advance, that strings are omitted entirely from Act II. There is enough to absorb his attention.

Then again, the music is not conceived in classic developmental terms. It proceeds by statement, counter-statement, thematic superimposition and juxtaposition—always reflecting precisely the psychology of the figures on stage. When Priam (in Scene I) remembers his own infancy—'So was I once a baby, born without choice'—the harp triplets heard earlier return. When Priam makes his choice—'The Queen is right. Let the child be killed.'—his proclamation is supported by Hecuba's violins. Together with this flexibility in the use of accompanimental motifs, there is an underlying unity of style. The opening prelude to the opera is both a symphony of war and an agonized image for the birth of Paris, dominated by off-stage trumpets and drums (joined by woodwind and piano) and vocalized cries from the female chorus (ex. 6). But the stark clusters of seconds and fourths which it features are really the key to all the music in the opera. This music returns in the outer scenes of Act II (with men's voices substituted in the chorus) for what Tippett calls 'minute formalized references to the fighting in the Trojan war . . . Troy will also go up in flames (in Act III) to a variant of the Prelude.'[36]

The linking of instrumental characters and stage personalities provide an important key to *King Priam*. The oboe, which

64

Act I of *The Midsummer Marriage* in the 1976 Welsh National Opera production

Act I of *The Midsummer Marriage* in the 1978 Adelaide Festival production with Carolyn Vaughan as Bella, Thomas Edmonds as Jack and Raimund Herincx as King Fisher

Act II of *King Priam* at the Royal Opera House, Covent Garden, in 1962
with John Dobson as Paris (foreground) and Victor Godfrey as Hector
(centre) Houston Rogers/Theatre Museum, London

Michael Tippett with David Atherton (conductor) and James Mallinson
(producer) at the *King Priam* recording session, November 1980

Clive Ba

ex. 6

in the opening scene signifies Paris in his cradle, follows him into boyhood in Scene II (when he is discovered by Hector and Priam during a hunting expedition, having been saved from death by a guard and raised by a shepherd); and then into manhood in Scene III (when he is enraptured with Helen); subsequently, it lends asperity to the woodwind writing that supports his arguments with Hector in Act II Scene I; and it is conspicuously missing when he assumes a war-like stance in Act III—he is now no longer Paris, the great lover (ex. 7).

Strings being absent from Act II, Tippett aptly chooses a guitar to transfer us into the intimacy of Achilles' tent. Here, the Greek hero sulks in the company of his beloved friend, Patroclus, singing him a song of nostalgia. The mood is enhanced by the sad tones of the cor anglais and two horns associated with Patroclus. When Achilles decides to allow Patroclus to fight Hector, aggressive writing for piano, percussion and horns takes over. All this is later recalled in Act III, when Priam comes to Achilles' tent to beg for the body of Hector.

There are other ingenious internal relationships that lend coherence to the brittle exterior of the score. The 'death' motif which follows upon the Old Man's reading of the dream in Scene I (two piccolos, xylophone, celesta, oboe and clarinet) recurs throughout the music associated with Hermes the messenger. In Act I, Scene IV, Hermes precipitates Paris into making the choice that is crucial to his father's future—the choice of one of the three Graces. The punctuation provided by xylophone and piano to his exchanges with Paris at the beginning directly recalls the 'death' motif. In Act II Hermes merely oils the progress of the war. In Act III his ironic nature comes to the fore as he presides over Priam's imminent death: he is a 'go-between' linking the world of the Gods and the world of men—he is 'between the inner world and the world of facts'. He interprets the final scene for the audience with a hymn to music. Finally, he appears as a God, as Priam awaits his end and, accompanied by the 'death' motif, sings of his awareness of only the inner world: 'I see mirrors myriad upon myriad moving the dark forms of creation.' Priam has entered the 'divine universe'.

King Priam hinges structurally upon its monologues. Most of these are the king's own. The first two counterbalance each other. Priam's decision, in Scene I, to kill his son is reversed in Scene II, when he discovers that his order was disobeyed and Paris has survived now into boyhood. 'In a moment of recognition' Priam accepts his fate. Here, and in the succeeding acts, the Nurse, the Old Man and Young Guard, and to some extent, Hermes, act as extensions of Priam's mind. Their ensembles partly comment on the action of the drama ('Life is a bitter charade' they sing between Scenes II and III in Act I); partly they signal a change of time and place (e.g. when the Old Man in Act II asks Hermes to take him to Achilles' tent and back); but, most important of all, they stem from Priam's monologues, helping us to keep in mind the viewpoint of the figure in the title role of the opera.

The climax of the probing of Priam's personality comes in Act III Scene II, when Paris has brought the news of Hector's death. Priam's long solo identifying his own fate with the tragic destiny of the world is developed as a dialogue with the Old Man, Young Guard and Nurse. Priam's world has collapsed. The last words of the Nurse—'Measure him time with mercy'—engender an orchestral interlude which, while it effects a change of scene, rivets our attention upon Priam's mental anguish.

Whereas Priam's monologues reveal his inner conflict in situations of choice, the monologues of the other characters exemplify in turn a more defined range of experience. All the male protagonists are absorbed with war. Hector and Paris are polar opposites—'once they knew they were brothers they never got on'—the former aggressively virile, the latter softly romantic: we watch Priam's efforts to reconcile and unite them in Act II. They are balanced by Achilles, unwilling to fight, and Patroclus who, 'in the nick of time' restores some manhood to Achilles. They are all brought into the great climactic ending of Act II, where Priam and his sons pray to the gods for assistance, and their prayer is interrupted by Achilles' blood-curdling war-cry—Patroclus having been killed—echoed by the chorus.

The female protagonists are given the stage at the start of Act III. Hecuba, as when she appears to Paris as Athene in Act I ('I will inspire you on the battlefield'), remains preoccupied with the war, public life, the fate of the city. Andromache, as when she appears to Paris as Hera in Act I ('I will give the warmth and trust within the marriage bond that is man's best reward if you honour me'), remains preoccupied with the home, her husband and children; in Tippett's words, she 'echoes down the centuries as the proud, passionate, grieving widow'.

Helen remains herself, the one character who has never to choose in any circumstances. Fatal in her involvements both public and private, she is faithful only to some mysterious, unavoidable passion. Insulted by Andromache—who sings, 'Go back to Greece, adulteress, and let this war be stopped'—Helen shows her true colours. No mere reflection of her husband, she can remind us of her divine birth—'for I am Zeus' daughter, conceived when the great wings beat above Leda'; love with Helen 'reaches up to heaven, for it reaches down to hell'. Helen's aria is the longest of the monologues for the female characters, and its style and substance—ornate lines and dancing rhythms allied to powerful rhetoric—make it comparable to Jenifer's aria, 'Then the congregation of the stars', in Act I of *The Midsummer Marriage*.

The scheme of proportions which underlies *King Priam* develops finally from the fact that all the main characters belong within a family and any movement out from that family has to be compensated by movement back towards it. On this point, Tippett takes his cue from Eric Bentley in *The Life of the Drama*, who postulates an 'original cast of characters in the drama of life, a drama that we keep on reviving later with more and more people cast for the same few parts'.[37] As in *The Midsummer Marriage*, Tippett is keen to investigate any archetypal dimension to his main characters. Here, he uses the device of divine origin or prototypes (with Hermes and the female characters); and the final climax of the work is concerned with a visionary perception of the inner life, in Hermes' hymn to 'divine music' and Priam's last words—'I see mirrors'. All this, however, has had to be placed carefully within an opera primarily emphasizing immediacy and actuality.

Actuality is virtually ignored in *The Knot Garden*. In this opera we focus exclusively on the inner life of seven individuals. There is no plot. The action takes place within the span of a single day. Its presentation is disjointed like the cutting of a film: the pace is even faster than *King Priam's*, there are no transitions between scenes, only cinematic 'dissolves', marked by repeated appearances of purely schematic music. 'Non-music', the composer calls it, picking up a suggestion from Harrison Birtwistle.

Over all, both the libretto and music of *The Knot Garden* constitute a texture of allusions. The title itself is an allusion to the formalized gardens of French origin popular in Elizabethan times, usually made of tiny box-hedges and low shrubs, and intended to relate the layout of the garden to the architecture of the house it adjoined. It could be thought of as a maze, or as a rose-garden in which, according to Persian tradition, lovers meet. Here, the action of the entire opera takes place in a garden which 'changes with the inner situations'—and in the central act it is explicitly a maze.

As in *The Midsummer Marriage*, the characters of *The Knot Garden* have names with appropriate resonances. The Latin origin of Faber's name—man, maker, engineer (according to Caesar)—pinpoints his preoccupation with practical everyday concerns. By contrast, Thea—her name is Greek for a goddess—is absorbed within the privacy of her garden. Their habit of retreating within their respective outer and inner worlds has caused their marriage to founder. Their young ward, Flora, still a 'flower'—an adolescent and a virgin—is obsessed with the half-real, half-imagined sexual threat of Faber. Mangus (a variant of the Latin *magnus*, meaning great) is the analyst who has been invited to sort out Flora's problems. He is quickly aware that the true disturbance is the rift between Faber and Thea, but he, like the other characters, lives in a dream-world in which he is all-powerful and can manipulate everyone and everything around him. There are guests at the house too: Thea's sister, Denise (named after the martyr St Denys), a revolutionary; and a homosexual couple, Dov (from the Jewish for David—a musician in the Old Testament), a young white musician, and Mel (from a Latin term of endearment, meaning honey), who is a Negro writer.

The Knot Garden is, in its dramatic methods, not unlike Shaw's *Heartbreak House* or Edward Albee's *Who's Afraid of Virginia Woolf?* Replacing conventional narrative here is a series of mostly short-lived attempts at communication by pairs of characters on stage. Act I (Confrontation) shows their failure to communicate. In Act II (Labyrinth), where the garden becomes a maze, the characters pair off in a fast-changing sequence, attempting unsuccessfully to 'connect' and starkly exposing their loves and hates. In Act III (Charade), at the instigation of Mangus, they play a series of short charades on themes from *The Tempest*. This is the most complex act. Surrealism, incidentally present earlier, now comes to the fore. Patterns of reconciliation are initiated. None of the solutions is easy or absolute. There is a Mozartian epilogue, the cast lining up at the front of the stage to address the audience directly: and a coda which is in fact a new beginning. The point where the curtain falls in the opera is the point where the curtain rises in their lives (an idea taken from Virginia Woolf's novel, *Between the Acts*).

The operatic genre to which *The Knot Garden* belongs is that of Mozart's *Così Fan Tutte*. Mangus is certainly comparable to Don Alfonso, setting in motion a play of elaborate relationships amongst the characters. But Tippett's opera takes further than Mozart the emphasis on duets and trios as opposed to arias. In the profusion of short scenes—fourteen in Act I, nine in Act II and ten in Act III—we meet the characters in twos and threes rather than singly.

Undoubtedly the most important allusion in *The Knot Garden* is to Shakespeare: to his 'comedies of forgiveness' in general and to *The Tempest* in particular; to his illusionistic techniques; and to the pluralist features of his language. The opera is indeed the climax of Tippett's fascination with Shakespeare— whom he describes as 'absolutely universal . . . translated into every language that exists . . . an enormous cauldron which we pour things into and take things out of . . .'; quite distinct from, say, Racine, exemplifying the 'French purist mandarin element'[38] for whom the mixing of genres and linguistic ingredients would be abhorrent. The language of the libretto of *The Knot Garden* is a deliberate attempt at a counterpart to Shakespeare's language: compounded of an infinite number of tiny cross-references, a mixture of erudition and collo-

71

quialism, and exhibiting a richness which ensures that nothing can be taken just at face value. As such, it is probably his finest libretto.

At the start of the opera, we have—as in *The Tempest*—a storm. In Shakespeare, it is a magical storm, produced by Prospero; in Tippett's opera it is our point of entry into the psychic storm within which Mangus (lying on the couch) is the still point. As he steps out of the storm, and all is becalmed, he sings,

> '*So, if I dream*
> *It's clear I'm Prospero:*
> *Man of power.*
> *He put them all to rights.*'

The action of the opera is, on one level, a dream. At the same time, as Mangus discloses in Act III (quoting *Hamlet*), the purpose of the play is 'holding the mirror up to nature'— reflecting thus the inner world of the characters.

The storm motif—growing from a sequence of twelve notes played in octaves at the start by wind and strings, but in no way implying any dodecaphonic principle of construction— appears throughout the work in various transformations, and generates other musical material from its uneven pattern of diminished and augmented intervals. In Act II especially, it introduces the whirling (literally) of the characters within the maze. Its telescoped harmonic version in the scene between Denise and Mel (Act II, Scene VII) can be contrasted with the extended aria sung later by Dov to Flora (Scene IX), where the original motif has been expanded outwards, lyrically. The storm motif is always associated with Mangus's manipulative powers in relation to psychological disturbances: cf. in Act I, Scene VI, where he sings

> '*Or till the priest magician* . . .
> *What's the quote?*
> "*Attend, Miranda!*"'

again, in Scene X,

> *'Flora, come with me.*
> *We need more costumes.'*

It goes musically into reverse in Act III, Scene VII when Thea can at last sing of reconciliation with Faber ('I am no more afraid'); likewise, in the Epilogue, (Scene X), where the two of them are alone in the garden, and they put aside what they are doing, accept their own natures, imaginative and sensual, so uniting their desire and imagination within one another. Here, at the conclusion of the opera, the music culminates to a chordal aggregate made up of nearly all the notes in the storm motif (see ex. 8).

Within the dramatic framework of *The Knot Garden*, each personality carries almost equal status. There are no 'stars'. In *The Midsummer Marriage*, the psychological barriers to the union of Mark and Jenifer are removed symbolically within the Ritual Dances of Acts II and III. *The Knot Garden* is one entire ritual dance. Throughout the work, Tippett uses the metaphor of a dance to stress the interconnectedness of all human affairs. Shakespeare and Goethe are invoked at the end of Act III for this very purpose. The text quotes from *The Tempest*:

> *'Come unto these yellow sands*
> *Let's dance together each to each to all'.*

Here, also, Tippett elaborates upon a setting of this, and of one of his *Songs for Ariel*. The text also refers to Goethe's poem *Das magische Netz* (*The Magic Net*).[39] This describes a group of people dancing with a net, how one goes in and one goes out, and this becomes a vision of the world. Tippett, in the final ensemble, quotes

> 'We sense the magic net
> That holds us veined
> Each to each to all.'

Elsewhere, dances, either in the action itself or imaged in the music, often serve to encapsulate the mental state of characters. Faber (in Scene III) enters to a jauntily dancing trumpet tune that for Flora signifies sexual provocation (ex. 9). Left alone (Scene V) Faber muses on his marital breakdown, and the dance motif becomes coarsely distorted. It resumes its original form

ex. 9

as, defiantly, Faber leaves Mangus a message to tell his wife he has gone to work. In his subsequent exchanges with Dov (in Act I, Scene XII and Act II, Scene V) the same motif recurs; likewise, in his encounter with Denise (Act II, Scene II) where the motif is taken over by the clarinet, and with Flora (Act II, Scene III).

The arrival of Dov and Mel in Act I, and their interaction with Flora, Thea, Mangus and Faber, are turned into an elaborate charade with dances interwoven into the action. Flora hums to herself (Scene VIII) a children's counting-song, 'Eeny, meeny, miny moe', which in its corrupted American version ('Catch a nigger by his toe') is highly apposite as a prelude to the entry of Dov and Mel (Scene IX). For their affair is teetering on the edge. Taunts are the order of the day. The two of them, in fancy dress, are immediately transfigured as Ariel and Caliban, the former trying to 'hook' the latter. Then, standing stock still, they pretend to be Tweedledum and Tweedledee out of *Through the Looking Glass*, whereupon Flora automatically assumes the role of Alice. Introducing them- selves and their little game, they dance around Flora to a teasing tune, which later on will become plaintive and pathetic.

Thea and Mangus (Scene X) bring an air of reality into the proceedings ('Children at play'), but only instigate another more disturbing ritual. Mangus takes Flora away. 'The triangle-trio that is left survey each other as in a ritual dance': offering them each a cocktail, Thea 'like Circe draws Mel hypnotically, by implication sexually, into the garden'. Dov, left alone (Scene XI) howls like a dog—a general expression of human loss and heartbreak. Discovered thus by Faber, he tries to brave his embarrassment by repeating the dance and ditty scene with which he and Mel had introduced themselves to Flora. Faber's own sexual ambiguity comes to the fore. He is fascinated with Dov. The feeling is mutual. Thea and Mel return and the four characters freeze into a tableau, in which none of them can yet articulate their feelings: only Flora's excited announcement of the arrival of Denise breaks the tension.

The playful charade and dance routine with which Mel and Dov make their entrance in Act I becomes a wild and agonized song and dance number when, in Act II, they confront each other in the labyrinth (Scene VI). Dov, in Mel's view, is not pursuing a relationship with Faber that is based on deep human feeling. He is tempted 'by the manhood not the man'. Dov replies that 'the heart's my family', but is urged by Mel to discover himself more fully. Later on, in Act III, Scene VIII the dance and ditty from Act I, Scene XI are used by Dov (again cast as Ariel) to taunt Mel (cast as Caliban).

The catalyst to most of the action amongst all these characters is Denise. She is the last to appear on stage in Act I. Until then, none of the interplay of personalities has come to much. Denise enters (according to the directions) 'half-majestic, half-sinister. She is twisted or otherwise disfigured from the effects of torture . . . she entirely dominates the stage.' Her long aria, typified by angular melody, generates so much emotion in the others around her that some outlet is necessary. This again Tippett achieves through a ritual—a slow blues, with a fast boogie middle section; within this, everyone can express his or her standpoint. Mel begs not to be tormented so; Dov wants love or will leave things as they are; Flora remains searching for her identity, a 'little girl lost'; Faber asks for a simple avowal of love; and Thea retreats from him into her garden. Throughout it all, Mangus stays within his Prospero role—

> 'And my ending is despair
> Unless I be relieved by prayer
> Which pierces so, that it assaults
> Mercy itself, and frees all faults.'

Denise, the freedom-fighter, a woman of great moral purity and integrity, who has lived through suffering and torture, prompts the others in the opera to confront the unbearable realities inside themselves. Although she is rarely in the foreground in the second and third acts, her influence remains strong. Sharing with Thea her vulnerability towards men (Act II, Scene I) she is a source of strength to her. Denise then exhorts Faber (Scene II) to explore the 'secret self' within

77

himself which she knows she already possesses and which makes her so tough.

She is drawn to Mel (Scene VII) by his colour, as a representative of an oppressed people. In the course of their duet, the civil rights song, 'We shall overcome' achieves prominence in the orchestral accompaniment. 'As though hearing it in his mind', Mel joins in at 'O, deep in my heart', singing 'as though the words are forced from him'. Something archetypal has expressed itself through him. Only in Act III, Scene V is Denise suddenly unsure of herself. Faced with Mel's Caliban side—his sensuality, which he indicates has been fulfilled in a homosexual relationship—she leaves in tears. Mel follows, at Dov's prompting. Dov realizes he has played a puppet role to Mel, who in turn recognizes that he is for the time being 'black earth for white roses'. Denise eventually regains her assurance. Mel follows her out and Dov, wanting to follow Flora, who has departed alone 'radiant, dancing', is impelled to trail behind Mel and Denise.

The ritual games of this opera reveal all manner of ambiguities and unexpectedness in human behaviour. As the collision of personalities reach nightmare level in the maze, ostensibly the two weakest characters, Dov and Flora, are flung together. The scene that follows (Act II, Scene IX) is one of Tippett's finest inspirations. Dov cradles Flora in her distress. He persuades her to do what he, as a musician, would do—sing in alleviation of grief. She responds with Schubert's *Die liebe Farbe* (from *Die schöne Müllerin*)—orchestrated by Tippett— singing the first verse in German, then supplying a vocal obbligato to the second in English. Dov offers in return his own rapturous aria, full of nostalgia for his youth in California yet linking metaphors from European as well as American culture. In Tippett's scoring of the aria, the jazz and rock associations of the electric guitar are transmuted, so that over all we have a modern equivalent both of the European stage serenade, sung by lovers, and of the 'fabulous rose-garden' of this scene. Mel appears to remind Dov that he taught him that song for it stemmed from their self-inflicted emotional scars.

Musically, this scene is typical of the work in its expansion of a mosaic-scheme of thematic ideas, and in its hints of Ivesian collage. It is stylistically and formally the basis for an opera which is not about firm solutions but about open-ended possibilities. Mangus, himself, comes finally to realize the limitations to his power:

> *'Prospero's a fake, we all know that:*
> *And perhaps the Island's due to sink into the sea.'*

Like Prospero, Mangus must end the illusion:

> *'Now that I break my staff and drown my book.'*

Like the rest of us, he is foolish and fond, 'whistling to keep my pecker up'.

Tippett, throughout the opera, has shown his characters

> *'Whistling to a music*
> *Compounded of our groans and shrieks*
> *Bitter-sweet and wry*
> *Tender yet tough: ironic*
> *Celebration for that trickster Eros.'*

The affirmations of *The Midsummer Marriage* are not possible here. At the most, it is a question of whether

> *'For a timid moment*
> *We submit to love*
> *Exit from the inner cage*
> *Turn each to each to all.'*

The Ice Break takes on to a larger canvas the themes of forgiveness and reconciliation present in *The Knot Garden*. Tippett declares in the preface to the libretto that its subject is 'stereotypes—their imprisoning characteristics—and the need for individual rebirth' and asks for a high degree of surrealism in the presentation of the work. This is necessary if it is going to appear as more than just a documentary about contemporary life. As usual the composer wants to convey something not at all tied to particular identities, or to a particular time and place.

In a note in the score, Tippett says, 'The chorus is always anonymous, whatever group it represents. It must be masked in some form, not only to enforce anonymity, but so that the stage representation is unrelated to the singers' real bodies, in the sense that, for example, the traditional black and white minstrels might be played by Chinese. The masking is also necessary to show that stereotypes in general are in question, rather than any presently exacerbated example e.g. "black and white".'

Tippett preserves the cinematic method of *The Knot Garden*, here, so that the pace of the opera is very fast. In addition, he implies that the actions should be conceived as a *totality*. Instead of following a succession of scenes, indoors and out we must think of the action as containing both simultaneously. Again, the chorus provides the key. 'In a chorus scene the whole stage is occupied and any extant non-chorus scene totally submerged ... when the chorus goes, the non-chorus scene appears once more in progress.' The ever-present chorus serves to remind us of the world of stereotypes, aggressive and peaceful, from which the individual seeks rebirth.

Surrealism invades the music of the opera. Individual singers, choral groups and orchestral ingredients are heard off stage and in electronically amplified form almost as much as they are heard live on stage or in the pit. Discreet use of sound effects (for example, airport announcements) is possible for the creation of appropriate atmosphere. But the fullest dimensions to the score are realized in two over-powering archetypal sounds: 'one related to the frightening but exhilarating sounds of the ice breaking on the great northern rivers in the spring; the other related to the exciting or terrifying sound of the slogan-shouting crowds, who can lift you on their shoulders in triumph, or stamp you to death.'

This is the basis of an opera which is as steeped in irony and allusion as *The Knot Garden*. Again a mosaic musical scheme is applied; but additionally, the opera features an abundance of Ivesian collage, combining and superimposing diverse ingredients. From this comes a richness of musical texture without which the opera might seem threadbare. For Tippett has concentrated the content of *The Ice Break* very tightly.

Of the nine characters in the opera, three are subordinate roles: a Police Lieutenant; Luke, the doctor; and Astron, the Messenger—all making fairly brief appearances. Two others, Gayle and Olympion, never progress beyond stereotyped patterns of behaviour. They are killed off in Act II. Thus the main burden of the action is carried by the remaining four characters. They are the focal figures in a plot collating conflict of different sorts—racial, political and familial. The setting implied by the text seems to be American but the action could equally relate to some other city capable of exemplifying those conflicts in the most up-to-date manner: Belfast; Jerusalem; or Johannesburg.

All the conflicts are exposed in the tensely wrought exposition of Act I. Nadia waits with her son Yuri at the airport for her husband, Lev, a teacher who has been released after twenty years in prison camps: she emigrated with their baby son to a new world, and at last he is to rejoin her. Yuri's girl-friend Gayle, and her black friend Hannah, a nurse, are also waiting at the airport for the black 'champion', Olympion,[40] whose fans swarm everywhere.

The conflicts erupt as both Lev and Olympion arrive. Yuri has no feeling for his parents. Olympion identifies with black supremacy. Gayle offers herself sexually to Olympion to make racial amends; enraged, Yuri attacks Olympion, only to be felled by a blow. Confrontation is inevitable on all levels.

The exuberant chorus of fans in Act I becomes an aggressive mob of blacks and whites in Act II. Each is allotted a tribalized form of musical expression. The whites are characterized by an old Methodist hymn used in Ku-Klux-Klan meetings and sung in 'barber-shop' harmony, with an obbligato of wailing trumpets and bass drum. When the fighting is about to start, their leader plays what the composer calls 'the devilish fiddling that comes from Blue Mountain music'. The blacks are polarized against them with violent Voodoo-style dancing (led by a clarinettist). For Nadia, it is a vision of 'the Dance of Death whirling over the city' (Act II, Scene I). Within it, now, each of the main characters takes his or her place.

Yuri rejects his father's pacifism—'every guy has a gun'. Gayle rejects the dream of 'liberal charity' to which Nadia and Lev have clung. Both are drawn away (Scene II) into the masked white mob. Olympion, though intimately involved with the apolitical Hannah (Scene III), feels obliged to champion the blacks and leaves Hannah behind (Scene V) who searches within herself for some way of deepening her experience and thus making sense of the chaos and violence around her. The extended aria 'Stranger and darker', probing the 'blue night of my soul', is a high point, musically, in the score, and also dramatically crucial: for with Hannah lies the hope for rebirth and continuity in human existence; 'born free, she won't take a step into the mob, who only know negatives'. After the subsequent scenes of violence, in which Yuri is almost fatally wounded and taken to hospital, it is to Hannah that Lev turns. The sharing of their grief in the epilogue to Act II marks a turning-point in the opera.

In Act III chorus and individual characters are caught up in a series of metaphors for rebirth. The reconciliation of father and son is prefigured in Lev's reading from the end of Goethe's *Wilhelm Meister* as he sits at Nadia's deathbed. Hannah dispels Lev's confusion (Scene III) reflecting that in a world of ghettos there is struggle everywhere: rebirth from them must be the prime aim. Nadia fades slowly into a peaceful death, which comes after she has vividly remembered her childhood especially skiing in the forest and the sound of the ice breaking on the river.

Then, once more emulating *The Tempest*, Tippett introduces a masque-like episode (Scene V) set in a Paradise Garden. Here, 'seekers of all kinds, tough and tender, past, present and future' are preparing for a 'psychedelic trip'. At its climax, they have a vision of an androgynous messenger-figure, Astron (sung by two voices, mezzo-soprano and counter-tenor). His message comes from Jung: 'Dear friends, take care for the

Earth, God will take care for himself.' When they hail him as a hero, he mocks them: 'Saviour?! Hero?! Me!/You must be joking.' Astron's ironic response signifies the ultimate rejection of all gods, gurus and ideologies—the source of all conflict in our world, past and present.

Finally, in the hospital, Yuri is released from the plaster in which he is 'totally encased', at least metaphorically (Scene VII). It is like the final bringing to life again of the statue of Hermione in *The Winter's Tale*: 'Be stone no more.'[41] The chorus of 'seekers' now burst in to celebrate spring, rebirth, regeneration. Yuri is reconciled with his father (Scene VIII): the ice has broken. 'Chastened, together, we try once more,' he sings. But he is over-confident. As Hannah hints, and Lev confirms, conflict will always recur, likewise its resolution:

> *'Yet you will always be brought forth again,*
> *glorious image of God*
> *and likewise be maimed, wounded afresh*
> *from within or without.'*

Goethe has had the last word.[42]

Not unexpectedly, given its subject matter, *The Ice Break* is one of Tippett's darkest scores. The violence of confrontation and regeneration are summed up in the grinding chords, low down on brass and percussion, followed by a motif which plays rhythmically with minor thirds, then major thirds: the ice break motif (ex. 10). This motif provides a sinister under-

current to the whole of the opening scene. Its musical material is subsequently expanded but returns more than once in its pristine form, for instance, at the first meeting between Lev and Nadia (Act I, Scene VII) where it is combined with another important chordal theme—the two of them figuring prominently in Nadia's death scene (Act III, Scene IV) and in the reconciliation between Lev and Yuri (Act III, Scene IX).

Tippett produces cohesion within the score by crystallizing motifs and their development in a variety of harmonic conflations of the notes they use. Chordal passages—whether decorated or not—always sum up the expressive content in the arias that they surround: for instance; in the introduction to Hannah's aria in Act III, Scene V, where the music flowers melodically (see fig. 14)* and reaches apex points on particular words, such as 'alone', where the accompaniment builds to a chordal aggregate. The conflicting major and minor thirds in the ice break motif are used extensively in this way—in Act I,

---

* Fig. numbers refer throughout the book to the *rehearsal figures* in the published scores of Tippett's compositions.

Scene VIII, where Lev remembers his political sufferings in Russia; and again at the very end of the opera. The technique is a further refinement of the processes encountered previously in *The Knot Garden*. Extensive percussion and two electric guitars—reinforce the effect of grim irony produced by the prevalence of the ice break motif and other comparable motifs. Whereas Hermes, in his hymn to 'divine music' can assuredly introduce a radiant vision to the tragic last act of *King Priam*, Hannah's aria in Act II hardly takes us away from harsh realities. The scoring of the accompaniment in each is worth noting (ex. 11): Hermes is supported by flute and harp; Hannah by flute and electric guitar. Luminosity yields to tenebrosity.

ex. 11

the whole chord sustained until

Hannah is the one character in *The Ice Break* who is allowed to flower fully into an identifiable personage. She, of course, avoids involvement in stereotyped behaviour. It is probably a weakness of Tippett's method that a number of figures here are only the sum of their parts. Their various traits are not fused, their private and public behaviour do not coalesce. They are in part prisoners of Tippett's theme: the old must die (hence Nadia's apparently gratuitous death in Act III) and the young must experience the conflicts and tensions of the plot within their own generation. In *The Ice Break*, also, the characters do not move with such fluency and freedom across the frontiers separating their actual selves from mythological, dramatic and other prototypes. In this respect, *The Knot Garden* was a *tour de force*: the consummate example of Tippett's operatic method. Moreover, Tippett's mosaic technique in the music to the opera for once hinders the blossoming of his characters and subverts some of his dramatic intentions. The eruption of violence in Act II is done with expert precision: but the psychedelic trip in Act III needs more expansion to make its proper impact. Maybe if Tippett ever tackles another opera— and he has spoken of reviving the masque tradition, perhaps around a comic theme—he will utilize a new technique, synthesizing the lyrical effulgence of *The Midsummer Marriage* with the fast-moving, hard-hitting procedures of the other three operas.

The themes and preoccupations of Tippett's four operas are widely encountered in plays and films by his contemporaries (apart from the aforementioned Albee). It would not be hard to imagine a film like *The Warriors* (1979)—concerned with individuals caught up in gang warfare in New York—transformed into an opera like *The Ice Break*: certainly its opening sequence has a comparable surrealism of treatment. Tippett's music, of course, places him at an advantage. It could well be used, for instance, to breathe life into the characters in R. D. Laing's play *Knots* (1972): for otherwise they remain imprisoned in their creator's theories about the terrorism of inter-personal relationships. By comparison, everyone in *The Knot Garden* vibrates with personality. Again, with Snoo

87

Wilson's *The Pleasure Principle* (1973)—a play which centres upon an unspoken relationship between two characters, Robert (a businessman) and Gale, whose opposing ideas of pleasure prevent them from actually making love until the last act—the mechanics of moving from actual to archetypal behaviour would have been achieved more smoothly and more convincingly if assisted by *Knot Garden*-style music; especially in the scene where Gale dreams of Robert seducing her, Leda-like, as a swan (which entails a cardboard swan being wheeled on stage): here the bizarre could have become transcendently expressive.

Tippett's last two operas beckon towards the free interplay of ingredients characteristic of recent (so-called) music-theatre or mixed-media works. But although he has taken on board ideas and techniques from the musical, from television and cinema, he has never relinquished the operatic aesthetic he learnt from Eliot, which ensures the dominance of the music over all other elements in an operatic presentation. Tippett is unlikely to change in that respect. This is not surprising: for his strongly defined and characterful musical idiom was hard won, and it was from such a foundation that he felt able to write operas at all.

7 FORM AND FANTASY

TIPPETT HAS OFTEN TOLD aspiring composers who send him
scores and tapes that he could never give a truly objective
judgement upon their work. At best, he himself would learn
from them and maybe 'steal' their ideas. Just as the intellectual jackdaw in his make-up is always on the alert for
new pickings, so, musically, Tippett has seized a lot from other
men's music. A cursory examination of his work would
support this observation. However, the end result is never mere
eclecticism. The outside influences have only nurtured and
accelerated the development of the composer's own personal
idiom.

Two categories of musical stimulus have had an effect on
Tippett's work. Some musical experiences have provided the
composer with definite formal and stylistic models; others
have simply enabled him to pinpoint the sort of musical image
he needed to start or end a work, or for some specific part of it.
These latter influences are so numerous that he has sometimes
forgotten what they were or what role they played in shaping
his thought.

He described the genesis of his Second Symphony thus: 'The
exact moment when the symphony began was when listening to
a tape of a Vivaldi concerto for strings in C, while looking out
over the sunlit Lake of Lugano. I was specially moved in that
situation by some pounding Vivaldi C major bass arpeggios. I
knew them to be the beginning of a new orchestral work. I do

not any longer remember the Vivaldi arpeggios, but four pounding bass C's are in fact the notes that begin the symphony—and they return at the end of the work. Their function is not so much to establish any key, but to act as a kind of point of departure and return.'

Likewise, the poetic playing of Walter Gieseking at a rehearsal of Beethoven's Fourth Piano Concerto suggested the character of a piano concerto which Tippett wanted to create himself. A radio broadcast of Bruckner's Eighth Symphony (conducted by Bernard Haitink) helped him determine the scoring of his own Fourth Symphony: and the instrumental ending of Act II of *The Ice Break* crystallized in his mind on hearing the gentle final bars of the slow movement of Brahms' First Piano Concerto, played by Alfred Brendel at the Festival Hall in London. Gleefully, the composer has also recalled 'stealing' from the soundtrack of Walt Disney's *Snow White* the duet for high divided violins that introduces the tenor solo, 'The Boy sings in his Prison', in *A Child of Our Time*. All this only illustrates how certain external musical experiences helped him focus the possible directions his own music might take.

At the outset of his career as a composer, Tippett steered a fairly independent musical course. He was not in sympathy with the aspirations of Vaughan Williams towards a national school of composition rooted in English folk song. He rejected Elgar and many of the other late-romantic figures such as Mahler and Bruckner, though later he came to value and learn something from all three. He was at first drawn to Sibelius—perhaps under the sway of R. O. Morris—and this affiliation is clear from his (unpublished) Symphony in B flat (1933/4).

Tippett's true path took him in the direction of neoclassicism—but not of the kind associated with Nadia Boulanger and her pupils. Like Stravinsky, whom he soon grew to revere, he had a consuming interest in the music of the past. But this did not hinge upon attempts simply to revitalize past musical forms with new and personal harmonic and rhythmic traits. In Tippett's music, a variety of formal procedures collide and conflict, producing a dualism in his work that runs deep.

90

Tippett shares Stravinsky's belief—enunciated in *Poétique Musicale* (1942)—that music has its own ontology: that attempts to impose upon it, either in advance, or retrospectively, some descriptive or ideological content, can only undermine its effect and significance, indeed, will strike at its very roots. On the other hand, Tippett has often enough (for instance, in his Third Symphony) felt impelled to contradict the abstract ingredient in his work with music bearing an explicit message. His respect for past traditions, masterpieces and models has ultimately fomented internal creative opposition.

Tippett's strongest allegiance was, and still is, to Beethoven: and this drew along with it various other affiliations—to the Elizabethan madrigalists and to Purcell; to Stravinsky and Bartok; to jazz and all forms of vernacular music. Soon, it issued in a kind of tension in his make-up—between the exigencies of classic formal procedures and the lure of inventive fantasy, and this tension manifests itself in all his music up to the present day.

In all his early works, with the exception of *A Child of Our Time*, Tippett was preoccupied with the formal aspects of composition. From the start, the example that meant most to him, in this respect, was Beethoven. 'When I was a student,' he writes, 'I submitted entirely to the music of Beethoven. I explored his music so exhaustively that for a long time later on I listened to every other music but his.'[43]

Tippett's initial efforts at achieving formal mastery are exemplified in his first two string quartets and the Piano Sonata No. 1. These are worth some detailed examination. All three works contain sonata-style allegros in the manner of Beethoven though the siting of these movements in the overall scheme differs in each case.

In the String Quartet No. 1, it is the first movement (replacing, in the revised 1943 version, the opening two movements composed originally in 1936) that contains the kernel of the musical argument. This is offset by a slow movement of unbroken lyricism and a fugue, wrought in strenuous Beethovenian fashion. In the String Quartet No. 2, the sonata-allegro comes last in the sequence of four movements, indicating a determined shift of emphasis to the end of the piece. Within each of these sonata-allegros, the main thematic ideas are sharply contrasted. Tonally, too, they follow classical precedent, though Tippett plays noticeably upon tonal ambiguity as an expressive device. For instance, the finale of the Second Quartet opens with a theme in C sharp minor; yet when this is recapitulated its key-signature does appear to confirm that this was really a disguised F sharp minor, the key in which the movement closes (though there the key-signature happens to be E minor!). In fact, whilst the notes are the same, what we are *hearing* is a recapitulation of the opening theme a fifth lower: likewise, the second theme, originally in E flat major (fourth bar of fig. 73, *et seq.*), returns a fifth lower in A flat major, thus supplying symmetry to the tonal plan.

Significantly, this is the most emotionally 'stretched' movement of the quartet: so much so that some find it unconvincing. But here, and in the first movement of the First Quartet, Tippett was clearly pressing into service all that he had learnt from Beethovenian formal methods. Only thus could his most intense and wide-ranging expression be contained and articulated coherently.

This is the rationale that underlies all Tippett's technical growth. It is evident immediately in the First String Quartet where, instead of establishing tonal centres as such, he tends to glide round them, treating them as major reference points in the design; and again, later, when his harmonic language had become more empirical and more diversified. Beethovenian sonata-style presentation often recedes from the foreground of Tippett's musical thinking; nevertheless, the same relationship between his material and its usage tends to apply. Tippett's neoclassicism thus relates closely to his own creative needs and bears hardly a hint of archaism or academicism.

The Piano Sonata No. 1 (1938) illustrates how Tippett's early development was nurtured by the Beethovenian example. Tippett describes this as 'a young man's work with all the exuberance of discovery and creation which that commonly implies'.[44] First entitled *Fantasy Sonata*, it shows the young composer's invention in full flood, given the stimulus of various kinds of popular music. Its slow movement is explicitly based on the Scottish folk-song 'Ca' the yowes tae the knowes'; the rondo-finale has jazzy syncopations; and amongst the variations that form the opening movement is one imitating the sounds of Indonesian gamelan orchestras, which the composer heard on record.

But it is the scherzo—coming third in the sequence of movements—that pulls the musical design into shape. Its toughness of statement and inexorable forward momentum are poles apart from the discursive character of the other movements. Laid out as a sonata-allegro, it inherits from the first movement the characteristic octave clashes between right hand and left hand, expressing forcefully now a clash of tonalities. Tippett's simple, direct melodic patterns acquire also a Beethovenian terseness. Without a scherzo of this type, the sonata might have seemed an indulgent sprawl. Its inclusion now alerts the listener to *all* the dimensions of the work.

Reviewing the first recording and score of Tippett's Piano Sonata No. 1 and the score of this String Quartet No. 2, William Glock[45] rightly drew attention to the 'new sense of rhythm gained chiefly from a relationship with music outside the Viennese period and all that can be connected with it'.[46] Tippett's buoyant rhythms are an important idiosyncrasy in all his music. Their derivation is twofold: from folk music outside the Austro-German tradition, and from the techniques of the Elizabethan madrigal. Contact with the music of Stravinsky and Bartok before and after this time only reinforced his fascination with a type of rhythm conceived as a flow of unevenly distributed accents, as distinct from that type of rhythm which relies on regular metres. 'Additive' as distinct from 'divisive' rhythm: these are the terms Tippett uses (they come from the ethnomusicologist, Curt Sachs) to show the approach to rhythm that is implied. Additive rhythm became a powerful force within Tippett's music, determining the nature of his musical invention and implying the formal directions his music might take.

In his early works, it appears as a technical acquisition from the madrigalists and church composers of the Elizabethan era. For at the same time, Tippett's discovery of his own personal 'voice' hinges on his exploration of a predominantly linear musical texture. A good instance of this is the fugal final movement of the String Quartet No. 1—the first instance, in fact, of a systematic use of additive rhythm in Tippett's music. It is headed by a quotation from Blake's *The Marriage of Heaven and Hell*: 'Damn braces. Bless relaxes'. At its simplest, the musical texture resolves into two main strands—written out so that pairs of instruments play in unison or an octave apart: these register harmonic tensions that are also the springboard for a veritable stream of irregular metrical patterns (ex. 12). As a whole, the movement is probably just too

The key-signature of three sharps applies
throughout the quotation (ex. 12)

ambitious. For, with such a proliferation of rhythmic accents, there is only a slight chance of introducing lyrical contrast. When a new fugue-subject appears (one owing much to the influence of Stravinsky's Violin Concerto), the music still bounds forward in the same rhythmic vein.

Tippett's Concerto for Double String Orchestra (1938/9) and his String Quartet No. 2 both overcome this limitation. The Concerto contains little or no dramatic conflict. For here, another formal approach allies itself with the rhythmic and polyphonic traits that have come to the fore in Tippett's music: that of the fantasia (or fancy), as exemplified in seventeenth-century masters such as Purcell or Orlando Gibbons. At this stage Tippett had not actually heard the Purcell and Gibbons fantasias. But his own discovery of a natural alliance between polyphony and freely inventive music was confirmed later when he did hear them; and the models they provided rivalled those he had been following in Beethoven. The freedom to introduce new ideas and immediately argue them to their limits—this is just the possibility the composer craved, but he knew that it could run counter to the overall coherence of the music. In this concerto, he found the Purcellian disciplines by instinct.

The opening movement of the Concerto has a sonata-style *sub*structure. The real energy of the music, however, comes from its uninhibited invention, its eager play of counterpoint. Significantly, the two string orchestras in the piece are not so much opposed as complementary. Continuity and drive take precedent over the confrontation of opposing thematic ideas. Maybe the players themselves derive the greatest enjoyment from Tippett's endlessly varied string textures: this is one facet of the work that exerts an unending appeal and fascination. Tippett's formal grasp, meanwhile, is such that hints of sonata-style organization can be discarded from the rest of the Concerto. Beethoven's influence is uppermost in the slow movement, an elegiac song with a fugal episode as its middle section, for this movement is modelled on the second movement of Beethoven's String Quartet in F minor, Op. 95. The finale is at first glance a sonata-rondo, but the appearance of a 'new' theme near the end confirms a stronger affiliation with the methods of the seventeenth-century fantasy.

Doubtless, it is possible to detect strong resemblances between the thematic material of each movement of the Concerto, and even analyse its growth from two initial 'germ cells'—one appearing on each orchestra in vigorous octaves at the outset, the first orchestra with four quavers on alternating notes, the second in a strongly syncopated rhythm (ex. 13).

There is also a thematic figure embodying a rising sixth which first appears in the middle of the first movement, returns in the fugal episode of the Adagio, and in the opening bars of the finale (ex. 14). But we must beware of expecting too much

Act I of *The Knot Garden* in the 1970 production at the Royal Opera House, Covent Garden

Michael Tippett with Colin Davis after the première of the Third Symphony in 1972

Michael Tippett with the pianist, Paul Crossley, in San Antonio, Texas

The composer with the Lindsay String Quartet at the Queen Elizabeth
Hall, 2 January 1980

thematic consistency from Tippett: diversity is as important as unity in his work, and tangential discovery is as attractive to him as the rigorous cultivation of defined territory. What we can observe here is that Tippett's thematic invention stays within a zone where family resemblances can occur.

In both this concerto and the String Quartet No. 2, Tippett encountered difficulty in notating additive rhythms. (He had not been alone in that: Stravinsky, Janacek, Bartok and others experienced the same problems when writing down music which needed to feel improvised.) In the first movement of the Concerto, he uses an 8/8 time-signature for music whose basic pulse is *alla breve*, simply in order to group the quaver beats in different ways—sometimes 4 + 4, sometimes 3 + 3 + 2 (in which case he asks the conductor to give three beats in the bar)—and so on.

In his preface to the score of the String Quartet No. 2, he states that the first movement 'is partly derived from madrigal technique where each part may have its own rhythm and the music is propelled by the different accents, which tend to thrust each other forward. The bar lines are thus sometimes only an arbitrary division of time and the proper rhythms are shown in the notation by the groupings of the notes and by the bowings.' A different solution is adopted in the third movement where 'the bar lines correspond to the rhythmical accents of the music' and the time-signature changes throughout very frequently.

Numerous performances of Tippett's music have foundered on rhythmic misunderstanding alone. Until a new generation of musicians arrived in the Sixties and Seventies with direct experience of performing everything from madrigals to jazz— almost any music outside the Viennese tradition, in fact—many interpretations of Tippett's works were stiff and wooden in effect. Nevertheless, the rhythmic lilt that figures in Tippett's music is associated with its linear emphasis, for the two together enable him to modify classic sonata-style methods with the alternative practices associated with the fantasia.[47]

If we consider again the first three movements of the String Quartet No. 2, we find that none of them is strictly a sonata-style movement. The first movement preserves some sonata-features. But its real vitality stems from a well-balanced scheme of thematic statement and development, oscillating between tension and repose. Tonal conflict is incidental rather than dramatically crucial. The heartbeat of the music sounds within the play of four equal lines; and always the invention tends to offer up its underlying implications at once, rather than storing them away for special moments in the piece. The two central movements of the work draw from both Beethoven and Purcell: an agonized fugue replete with chromatic inflexions evokes both the late fugues of Beethoven (such as Op. 131) and Purcell's string fantasias; while Tippett's mercurial scherzo—ingeniously laid out as three statements of the same music, presented each time a third higher and subtly modifed at the second and third repetitions—pays homage to the Beethovenian scherzo and to pre-classical dance music. For a composer who had to struggle so hard to produce anything equal to his ambitions, these compositions sound amazingly effortless. Only when we recall how much work and imaginative effort they entailed can we measure Tippett's achievement in turning himself into a front-rank composer during his middle thirties.

In composition that attaches so much importance to sheer invention, whole works can stand or fall on the quality of the basic material or on its capacity for immediate extension and growth. The *Fantasia on a Theme of Handel*, for piano and orchestra (1939–41), for instance, falls between stools, failing to draw much sustenance from the original Handel chords (taken as quoted at the end of Chapter 5 of Samuel Butler's *Erewhon*). It too readily goes off at tangents—introducing the main motif of the finale of Mozart's *Jupiter Symphony* and suggestions of the *Dies Irae* theme. Neither Beethovenian nor Purcellian discipline exerts a strong enough influence on Tippett here: the Fantasia is not unattractive but its rhetoric tends to sound gauche and ill considered. In a safer, less ambitious miniature, the *Little Music* for strings (1946), Tippett preserves more self-control and the end result is ingratiating.

In the case of the String Quartets, Nos. 3 (1948) and 4 (1978), the model is again late Beethoven, though some sonorities are imported from Bartok. The Third Quartet is dominated by its fugues, which are highly wrought in the manner of those in the late Beethoven sonatas and quartets. Three quick tempo fugues here enclose two movements whose successive outpourings of lyricism bring the work to its emotional apex: again, a characteristic late-Beethoven scheme, as also is the sense that each movement belongs with the others in a continuous sweep of music. Tippett has sought to emphasize this continuity by recently asking for the fourth and fifth movements to be linked without a break in performance. The finale thus begins on the last chord of the fourth movement.

Late Beethovenian imagery figures prominently in the Third Quartet. Thus, Tippett's musical material often burgeons into decorative patterns in short notes or it dissolves into ecstatic trills. We meet all this straight off in the introduction to the first fugal movement, whose slow-moving chords are quickly lost amid a welter of demisemiquavers, growing directly from a viola motif in the third bar. Out of this, also, develops the first fugue subject—one whose dimensions relate it to the fugue subject of the finale of Beethoven's *Hammerklavier Sonata*. The magnitude of Tippett's fugal thinking in this movement is such that he has time to recall the slow introduction as a momentary episode of repose in the structure. Even more virtuoso as a piece of fugal writing is the third movement. Although this has two subjects, there is little or no dramatic tension. Tippett's effervescent, dancing music encourages the listener to imagine that all four players are merely improvising together (though in fact they are clinging on to the written notes for dear life!).

Some of Tippett's most spontaneous-sounding musical invention is cast here within two rigorously planned fugal movements. By contrast, there seems hardly any check on the lyrical efflorescence of the second and fourth movements. Their formal simplicity is deceptive: Tippett adeptly applies fantasy techniques to song form. His skill is manifest in the second movement, in the way the four statements of the main theme—on first violin, second violin, viola and cello in

99

succession—are presented; and in the way the introductory motif returns half-way through and closes the movement. The fourth movement virtually proceeds on intuition—a daring which only an accomplished fantasy-composer could allow himself. It consists simply of three statements of thematic material of similar character and shape, starting in motionless music and gradually culminating in pace, power and rhetoric.[48] As in many late Beethoven quartets, the finale brings us gently back to earth. Although rich in ideas, this fugue is essentially simpler: its end is undoubtedly predicated by its beginning.

Contemporary critics of Tippett's first three quartets slighted them on account of their being too slavishly Beethovenian. Rarely, however, does semi-pastiche intrude upon any of his work. Only when Tippett consciously embarks on music 'written to order' does he sometimes fail to fuse any 'stolen' material with his own ideas. This is partly true of the Suite for the Birthday of Prince Charles and of the *Divertimento on Sellinger's Round*, despite occasional glimpses of the composer's personal idiosyncrasies. In the Divertimento, the Sellinger dance tune is combined, during the five movements, with ideas lifted from Gibbons, Purcell, Arne, John Field and Sullivan. But only in the fourth movement, which has echoes of *The Midsummer Marriage*, do we abandon a sense of miscellany in favour of a single thread of thought.

A work which at first might only seem to genuflect before its original model is the *Fantasia Concertante on a Theme of Corelli* (1953). However, the content and methods of this piece activated Tippett's deepest creative impulses. He discerns in the original Corelli a kind of archetypal Italianate lyricism. 'The most fascinating thing about the theme,' he notes (it is taken from Corelli's Concerto Grosso op. 6 No. 2 in F), 'is that, if Corelli's bass in F minor is put into the relative major of A flat major and somewhat extended, it produces a melody of pure Puccini!' This is precisely what Tippett does for a lyrical episode in the middle of the Fantasia (figs. 39–46).

Tippett also provides a counterpart for this effulgent strain of melody in the concluding pastorale section (which echoes Corelli's pastorale style in the so-called *Christmas Concerto*). Thus

100

is Corelli's music subtly transmuted into an ardent Tippettian vision of human rapture and natural beauty.

The general format of the Fantasia also recreates the characteristics of the original in Tippett's own terms. Corelli's division of the orchestra is emulated in the tripartite layout of *concertino* (two violins and cello), *concerto grosso*, and *concerto terzo* (a section of the string orchestra playing, at first, the continuo role, but later regarded as equal to the *concerto grosso*).

Rather than blandly lifting a theme from Corelli, Tippett structures two segments from the original to sustain sharp contrasts of passion and brilliance. He takes Corelli's short contrapuntal *adagio* theme and tacks on to it a *vivace* passage, all on the one chord of C major. These are the polarities that form the basis of the subsequent variations and fugue. Then again, we find that the fugue embodies a transcription the composer has made of the opening of Bach's Fugue in B minor (BWV. 578) for organ, itself based on Corelli themes. With hindsight we might regard this as an odd prefiguration of the medieval parody techniques revived in the music of Peter Maxwell Davies and others.

Close acquaintance with the *Fantasia Concertante* shows how completely Tippett has drawn into his own domain Corelli's musical ideas. The other strong feature of the piece is its bounteous lyricism, inherited from *The Midsummer Marriage*. Remarkable, indeed overpowering, is the way Tippett embellishes the fugue with swirling decorative lines that carry it to an overtly erotic climax, subsequently detumescent in a pastorale section stylistically related to the final dawn chorus music from *The Midsummer Marriage*. The *Corelli Fantasia* attains a rapture and perfection rare in music.

Sonata and fantasy are not invariably reconciled in Tippett's mature music. Indeed, it could be argued that only in his late works, such as the Fourth Symphony, has he managed to have the best of both worlds. When he embarked upon the composition of symphonies and concertos, Tippett was naturally impelled to modify established notions of content and format. Thus, in his First Symphony (1947), the slow movement is a passacaglia based on an eight-bar theme (introduced by bassoon and strings), which is repeated beneath, or in conjunction with, a variety of musical material; and the finale is a Beethovenian double-fugue.

In the first movement, though, fantasy and sonata collide. No fewer than six thematic groups make up the exposition. Their conception is linear. This emphasis on polyphony throughout the movement distracts from any attempted sonata-style development. Since, too, the ideas themselves are not Tippett's most inspired—neither fertilized by any other music, nor striking off in a direction avowedly their own—the movement as a whole hangs fire. An additional insecurity stems from the uneasiness of the scoring. Tippett writes polyphon-'ically for an orchestra whose internal balances were conceived originally for the vertical harmonic schemes of the Viennese masters. Many gestures in the first movement fail to register. No wonder: Tippett and Brahms make strange bedfellows!

Fortunately, Tippett's invention takes wing in the other movements. His scoring—including, notably, three flutes doubling three piccolos, double-bassoon and three trumpets—begins to tell. Especially felicitous are the exchanges for muted trumpets and horns, followed (after a theme for three flutes) by further exchanges between piccolos and brass, in the slow movement (3 bars before fig. 5–fig. 6). These breathe the same rarefied atmosphere as the closing scene of *The Midsummer Marriage*, the opera Tippett was about to compose. Other idiosyncratic strokes, uniting strong invention and exact orchestration, are the sudden intrusion of the bass-drum and trills for woodwind and violins in the finale, heralding the close of the work.

According to Tippett, the scherzo owed its particular character and format to some Pérotin vocal trios he had heard. In these, 'after a few measures of plainsong in quarter-notes, the voices took off in a flying hocquet on a chosen vowel in bumpy eighth notes'.[49] When challenged, the composer admitted not being able to describe with certainty an authentic medieval hocquet. Moreover, hocquets don't fly. At best, we can treat his terminology merely as a graphic description of the rhythmic 'hiccuping' that occurs throughout this scherzo—which is in essence a vivid recreation of the one-in-a-bar presto movement of a Beethovenian scherzo, with a trio in duple time. In the main body of the scherzo, the full orchestra tends to be used mainly for punctuation and as a means whereby the various musical strands can be drawn together into the cadential phrases that end each clearly defined section. Much of the musical argument centres upon exchanges between contrasting groups of wind and strings, with the harmony mainly in three parts, though sometimes four or two parts. The trio, on the other hand, is a freely unfolding string fantasy.

Already Tippett had had to reconsider not only the formal and thematic aspects of large-scale orchestral compositon, but also the important matter of colour. This reappraisal continued with far-reaching effects.

Tippett's Piano Concerto (1955) appears on the face of it to emulate the standard nineteenth-century opposition of soloist and full orchestra, but it splits up the orchestra to create a more varied dramatic canvas. In the sonata-style first movement, the solo piano and full orchestra occupy the foreground, but Tippett adds an extra evocative dimension with an ensemble which consists of solo viola, celesta and muted horns. This use of the celesta, in particular, is an extension of the pianist's most ethereal sonorities: thus Tippett can achieve the poetic intimacy which he wanted to reproduce from Beethoven's Piano Concerto No. 4—which is our abiding impression of the work. We encounter these ethereal sonorities again in the rondo-finale, where the third episode introduces—in contrast with the main gigue-like theme—a duet for piano and celesta (ex. 15, p. 104).

Tippett's attention to his colour scheme actively sustains the formal coherence of the concerto. Without it, the structure could become enmeshed in a thicket of decoration. The listener can succumb here to what, in musical terms, might seem to be a changing vista of luxuriant natural scenery; or equally, might recoil from its apparent narcissism. Both views are superficial. Tippett chooses his notes and mixes his colours

with equal care. In the slow movement, for instance, some elements of the conflict between piano and orchestra in Beethoven's equivalent slow movement have been taken over and imaginatively transformed. The pianist pours out an almost endless stream of arabesques which wash around continuous canons for the wind instruments (supported by lower strings). Throughout all this the violins and violas are silent. But then, shortly before the close, they enter with a burst of passionate rhetoric to which the pianist opposes his own ruminative reflections—and these remain finally in the ascendant. From such a bald description, it might seem a simple ploy: yet amid the proliferation of notes, it ensures an exact outcome for the movement. It also typifies this composer's clear-sightedness in extracting a particular point from a mass of detail.

Like the *Corelli Fantasia*, the Piano Concerto owes much to *The Midsummer Marriage*. The opening theme of the concerto, for example, is a clear offshoot of the music in Act III of the opera for the continuation of Sosostris' aria (fig. 387 *et seq.*). The tintinnabulations achieved with celesta as a prominent instrument in the outer movements most obviously relate to the 'temple' music in the opera (see ex. 3 above). But the horn writing here, and in the Sonata for Four Horns (1955) echoes, through the whole of Tippett's music. So we must beware of drawing boundaries around groups of works when they so often overlap.

The radical re-thinking of the role of the orchestra necessitated by the composition of the opera, *King Priam*, did not mean that all Tippett's past fund of imagery was being discarded. The coda for horns in the slow movement of the Second Symphony and the hunting scene of Act I in the opera contain music manifestly related to the Sonata for Four Horns and the Piano Concerto. Nevertheless, Tippett's new 'mosaic' orchestration for the opera, built from a repertoire of instrumental 'characters', marks a definite departure from his previous modes of composition: one in which Beethovenian processes are in abeyance, if only temporarily.

The fresh concept of orchestration and tautness of construction that are the hallmarks of the opera are foreshadowed in Tippett's Symphony No. 2 (1957), especially in the slow movement. The song format of this movement runs in close harness with a symmetrically balanced scheme of instrumental groupings. Sonata-style development is absent. Instead, we have a pattern of restatement and recapitulation (sometimes fragmentary) whose transformations of thematic material fundamentally affect its colour and register. The two themes which we predominantly hear are an introductory trumpet solo and a heavily ornamented duet for divided cellos. These are both recapitulated a tone higher, but with different instrumentation and in a different register. The trumpet motif is taken over by a trombone: the cellos relinquish their theme to divided violins. With the latter theme, also, the spread woodwind chords that accompany it are transferred to trombones—stalactites changed to stalagmites, as it were. Three elements of continuity appear within these changing patterns of colour and texture. One is the presence of the piano and harp, supplying incidental punctuation and embellishment. The others are an extended theme for the entire string orchestra, and its preceding trumpet fanfare to which the rest of the orchestra reacts promptly. These are only brokenly recapitulated at the end: the mosaic shatters and we are left with a mysteriously evocative coda on four horns—a colour absent from the mosaic-scheme until now.

In the rest of the symphony we find a further tightening up of Tippett's symphonic methods. Although the initial inspiration for the opening movement and its pounding C's came, as we noted earlier, from Vivaldi, the real exemplar for the symphony as a whole is Stravinsky's Symphony in Three Movements (1942/5). Its ethos of ritualized violence balanced against a lambent lyricism, is here made part of Tippett's world. Tippett noticeably copies Stravinsky in including a piano in his score, on account of its rhythmic and percussive character and its timbre; and with each symphony the central tonality of the outer movements is C. Yet Tippett provides his work with an identity of its own.

The first movement is Tippett's most assured sonata-style movement to date, with all the material trenchantly delivered, its overall proportions firmly conceived and with an inexorable driving motion from first to last. The third movement has been described by the composer as, 'A kind of mirror form scherzo, whose undeviating idea is the play between long beats (of three quavers) and short beats (of two quavers). The climax of the movement is where this play is closest and most abrupt [i.e. fig. 105 et seq.]. The beginning and end are on the other hand gentle and cool.' This movement is a sophisticated use of additive rhythm as the basis of a musical structure. By contrast, the finale is the oddest and least secure movement. It embodies a passacaglia (which gets underway after the balletic Stravinskian gestures of the introduction) and a return to the pounding C's of the opening movement. The link is an idiosyncratic digression—a long tune in A flat major, starting high up on the violins and descending very gradually into the depths, accompanied by brilliant *Petrushka*-esque 'blazes of colour' (as the composer calls them) on wind, harp and piano.

On paper, this might seem an imaginative way of rounding off the work. But the final pages rarely sound convincing. To emulate at this point the tonal argument of the first movement is risky, for there is insufficient room for it to expand. In the opening movement an intricate pattern of tonal tensions had been wrought from the conflict between sharp and flat keys, both of which seek resolution in the neutral home key of C major. This conflict is initiated in the opening theme by the playing off against each other of C major and D major (ex. 16);

and then by a second subject group beginning in A flat. It is brought to the fore in the central development section and continued in the recapitulation and long Beethoven-style coda. When Tippett harks back to all this in the finale, he tries to contain the tonal conflict within a series of sharply polarized thematic gestures, in opposition to the pounding C's. The final resolution—in which the trumpet flattens its G sharp to G natural and plays the notes of the C major triad—is premature and almost gratuitous (ex. 17, p. 108). It makes the tonal argument seem too generalized, too pithy. While this was clearly the stage at which the musical argument needed clinching, a subtler method of achieving it was needed. Concluding a composition has always given Tippett trouble. He never liked emphatic cadences of a traditional cast, and recoils from the bombast found in Walton, Shostakovich and others.

Ultimately, the uncertain technique of this finale is best regarded as a symptom of fundamental structural changes that were to occur in Tippett's music with *King Priam*. His retrospective comments on this change are indeed apposite. 'The dramatic processes demanded for this opera forced me to reconsider the standard orchestra radically. I began to realize

ex. 17

that the sound of the standard orchestra has become so strong
that contemporary music written for it gets inevitably drawn
back in history by analogy to the period when the archetype
was produced ... I realized that the use of the string body
within the standard orchestra was for me the crux. For this
body is historically the string quartet blown up, so that there is
a terrific historic archetype embedded within it. I was at least
ready to let go of this archetype and replace it with a body of
string instruments whose number and layout would be entirely
conditional on the piece to be composed. Essential to this
understanding was the realization that there were to be no first
or second violins, but just violins...'[50] This is the outcome in
the mosaic scoring of *King Priam*.

The overflow from this opera into other works has been
considerable. Directly derived stylistically and structurally from
the opera are the Piano Sonata No. 2 (1962) and Concerto for
Orchestra (1963), both of which contain actual quotations
from the opera. Immediately, in the sonata, we find that

sonata-style methods have been almost entirely abandoned. The fantasy procedures of Purcell and Gibbons are given a new lease of life. Tippett's musical thought flows uninhibitedly within a more concentrated, tightly organized format. 'As in the opera,' the composer tells us in his programme note, 'everything in the sonata proceeds by statement. The effect is one of accumulation—through constant addition of new material, by variation and repetition. There is virtually no development and particularly no bridge passages. The formal unity comes from the balance of similarities and contrasts. The contrasts are straightforward ones of timbre and speeds. But there are also contrasts of function. Music can appear to flow; or to arrest itself especially through the devices of *ostinato*; or temporarily to stop in silence... Because the work is for one player and one instrument there is little opportunity for the "climax " of a "jam session", i.e. when the contrasting sections or bits from them, instead of being just sequential, are made to appear together. These "climaxes"... are more appropriate to an orchestral piece in this form. But the sonata nevertheless has a kind of "climax" coda where the bits of addition and repetition are made very small and the resulting mosaic therefore more intense.'

The table below shows the kind of format with which Tippett was experimenting. We find him defining the elements in the sonata in terms of tempo indications: these recur in the score every time the material in question is altered, extended or contracted. There are thus eight main sections to the work (A–H). Looking at the table, we observe that the last section (H) has the greatest number of tiny components: this is the point at which listeners readily appreciate the mosaic character of the music—the 'climax' coda referred to earlier.

Section A presents the opening sequence of five thematic ingredients. Sections B, D and F contrast the relaxed, Chopinesque semiquaver patterns of Tempo 4 with other, more aggressive ideas encountered previously. Section C introduces new material—a set of four tiny motifs, repeated six times in the same order, with modifications. Section E also introduces a new motif whose two simple components are juggled about at

Piano Sonata No. 2

Section	Musical Material with associated Tempo Indications	No. of bars
A	1 (Lento ♪ = c. 100)	4
	2 (Allegro ♩ = c. 112)	3
	3 (Molto piu mosso ♩ = c. 200)	7
	4 (Pochissimo meno mosso ♩ = c. 138)	7
	5 (Adagio ♩ = c. 54)	8
B	4	12
	5	4
	4	15
	2	8
C	6 (Andante ♩ = c. 58)	67
D	3	7
	4	5
	3	7
	4	8
	5	12
E	7 (Allegro ♩ = c. 132)	33
F	4	18
	2	8
	3	7
G	8 (Lento ♩ = c. 40)	9
H	2	9
	3	7
	4	2
	6	2
	7	3
	6	2
	7	1

6	1
4	4
7	2
6	2
7	2
6	2
3	4
8	2
7	4
3	3
1	16

different pitches; while section G interpolates a new idea whose dramatic function is to set in motion the final 'collecting up of pieces'.

The harsh chordal rhetoric of the opening only reappears in the final page. This can give the piece a cyclic feeling. But, in fact, the quiet music polarized here against the violent chords draws our attention also to the resemblances between much of the thematic material in the work, which tends to focus upon intervals of major and minor seconds and ninths (see ex. 18).

Tippett's Concerto for Orchestra[51] compensates, to some extent, for the abrasiveness of *King Priam* and the Piano Sonata No. 2. While using the same building block methods of outlining its structure, and the same type of orchestration as we find in the opera, it allows more scope for sheer lyricism.

Its first movement, in some ways the most original, is based upon nine thematic 'blocks', each individually scored: and within these we find that music emphasizing 'line and flow' is allotted equal importance alongside music that is ostensibly 'heroic or martial', or which overtly stresses 'speed and energy':

A   1   Flutes and harp
    2   Piano and tuba   }   line and flow
    3   3 horns

B   1   Timpani & piano
    2   Oboe, cor anglais, bassoon and
        contra-bassoon   }   heroic and martial
    3   Trombones and percussion

C   1   Xylophone and piano
    2   Clarinet, bass-clarinet & piano   }   speed and energy
    3   Trumpets & side-drum

In the exposition of these nine ideas, each group of three is linked to the next by a few bars superimposing fragments from the three ideas just introduced (e.g. A is linked to B with a few bars of A 1, 2 and 3 heard simultaneously—see ex. 19).

Michael Tippett assisted by Sergeant Martin at his seventieth birthday celebrations at the Royal Opera House, Covent Garden, in July 1975

A page from the manuscript score of *The Mask of Time*

113

Thereafter, the entire movement is composed of juxtapositions of all this material, or extensions of it.

We could call the three subsequent stages in the movement 'development' sections, but we should refrain from doing so, for that might imply a connection with sonata-style methods that are foreign here. The movement is digestible because the subsequent extension and super-imposition of the musical material are offered to the listener in three stages. The opening theme for flute and harp acts as a signpost: and this is another deftly managed operation, for the theme itself is in three sections, and each time we return to it, we begin at its three distinct entry points.

We should note here, too, that the opening theme is a close relative of the accompaniment to Hermes' aria in Act III of *King Priam* 'O divine music', (see ex. 11) and thus represents the most powerful impulse towards lyricism within the movement. By contrast, the character of the second thematic group (B) is summed up in its final motif (B 3), derived from the Young Guard's encounter with King Priam in Act III of the opera (fig. 455 *et seq.*). The 'speed and energy' of the third thematic group arise in more general terms from Act II.

Undoubtedly the most unusual facet of the concerto is its 'open-ended' character. Although the first movement reaches a climax, marked by a gong-stroke (a sound not previously heard in the piece), and then subsides, it reaches no definite conclusion or cadence. We are meant to go on hearing the various instrumental *concertini* combine and juxtapose in our minds long after the musicians have stopped playing. This is consistent with Tippett's attempt to emulate on an abstract level the re-thinking of the orchestra that occurred in *King Priam*: for we go away with a fragmented impression of its range of colours, instead of recollecting homogeneous aspects—rather as we might recall the blend of colours in the closing *tutti* of many nineteenth-century symphonies.

A similar sense of renewal is achieved in the second movement, where the strings—a small body, according to Tippett's specification—play for the first time, along with piano and harp. Here, too, the rather short-breathed impact of a mosaic design is offset by a long continuous cantilena melody of the kind favoured by eighteenth-century composers when writing the middle movements of their concertos. The melody forms a central thread to which other motifs supply accompaniment. It starts with cellos high up and works its way down to their lowest note; then the violas take it towards the heights again, whereupon the violins continue the music even higher. At their highest point, the cellos recapitulate their long melody below.

During the composition of the concerto, Tippett fell ill. Anxious to complete it in time for its première at the 1963 Edinburgh Festival, he hurried through the composition of the final movement. His haste shows. The finale combines uncertainly the mosaic style methods of the earlier movements with rondo form, using more extended thematic ideas. Unfortunately, its effect is piecemeal. The ideas are not as cleverly planned and presented as in the first movement. Tippett quotes themes from Act II of *King Priam* (including one which is featured also in the Piano Sonata No. 2 as its Tempo 2 idea—see ex. 18) and these form merely a context within which the main rondo theme (for trumpet and violins), and the slow interludes, dominated by a theme for flute and bassoons in canon, can disport themselves. But this finale dissipates its inventive resources.

Just as Tippett's sense of discomfiture with the 'standard' orchestra had led him to re-think the layout and balance of the instrumental forces needed for his compositions of the late Fifties and Sixties, so he had had to re-define symphonic composition in terms which would satisfy his urge to invent freely against a background of classic forms.

He has rationalized his attitude to the symphony thus: 'The two contrasting conceptions or ideas of what is meant by a symphony are: that we imply by the title a *historical archetype* (from which we depart and return), e.g. the middle symphonies of Beethoven; and that we imply a *notional archetype* (permitting endless variations to the end of time), e.g. the Mahler symphonies, as variations of a notional archetype, are as much symphonies as those of Beethoven (irrespective, of course, of pure value judgement). It is then surprising how easily we can say almost in the same breath that the Mahler symphonies are not true symphonies at all, because they do not conform to our historical archetype of the moment, and then say that Mahler gave the symphony a quite new and valid form, because we momentarily abandon the conception of a historical archetype for that of a notional archetype.'[52]

Given this terminology, Tippett's first two symphonies are clear instances of the historical archetype: abstract works of a 'neo-classic' character. In his Third and Fourth Symphonies (dating from 1972 and 1977, respectively), Tippett manages to accommodate both archetypes.

The historical archetype in Symphony No. 3 is what Tippett calls the 'famous hybrid work'—Beethoven's Ninth Symphony: hybrid, because it moves from abstract instrumental music to vocal music bearing an explicit message. So fundamental is the Ninth Symphony to this work that Tippett felt he could only cross over into his vocal finale by quoting Beethoven's raucous presto opening to his own finale. Tippett's subsequent vocal blues and instrumental 'breaks' are also a commentary upon Beethoven (and Schiller): a twentieth-century answer to late eighteenth and early nineteenth-century affirmations of joy and human brotherhood. The recitative passage for cellos and basses which introduced Beethoven's *Ode to Joy* variation theme and the theme itself are embedded in the texture of this movement, and subject to a kind of dismemberment. Such procedures are not unlike the creative re-appraisal of Beethoven found in Charles Ives (notably the *Concord Sonata*). There is an interesting parallel, too, in Bernd Alois Zimmermann's last orchestral piece, *Photoptosis*, composed roughly at the same time as Tippett's symphony (1968). Here, too, after an enormously dense climax, Beethoven's presto bars are quoted: the outcome, though, is very different—an attempt to draw order from a further collage of quotations from *Parsifal* and the *Nutcracker Suite* amongst others. What Zimmermann and Ives share with Tippett is a sense of the inescapable moral force within Beethoven's music.

116

At the same time, the notional archetype in Tippett's Third Symphony ensures its substantial impact. This produces the basic ground-plan for its 55-minute span of music: two large scale movements, the first combining opening allegro and slow movement, the second joining the scherzo to the finale. It is also evident in the internal construction, an ingenious reconciliation of mosaic and sonata-style treatments. On the one hand, Tippett's invention became more diversified in the years that separate this work from the major orchestral work, the Concerto for Orchestra. This is not surprising when one remembers that the symphony was preceded by *The Knot Garden* and *Songs for Dov*: also, at this time, Tippett began to travel considerably in the USA, and came to know some of Ives's music for the first time. On the other hand, his constructional methods became more assured, so that form and fantasy were now on an equal footing.

Tippett finds a parallel to his musical 'block-building' in Stravinsky; and, as with that master, the exact definition of ideas does not preclude the possibility of their development. In this work, Tippett discovers a way of generalizing his mosaic patterns so that their subsequent usage is not fragmentary. Part I has an opening movement based entirely around two categories of thematic material—what the composer calls 'Arrest' and 'Movement'. This stems from the original conception of the work, which began in Tippett's mind while he was listening to a performance of Boulez' *Pli selon pli* at the Edinburgh Festival in 1965. What he heard then was music that was very 'motionless': 'It hadn't a harmonic or rhythmic or any other sort of drive that I could hear.'[53] Recognizing that he could only ever use that kind of musical gesture for expressive purposes if it were part of a piece based on sharp contrasts, he suddenly realized that such a division could be the foundation of a symphonic work. 'Arrest' means a 'compression of energy'; 'Movement' means an 'explosion of energy'.

Thus the whole of the opening movement in Part I is based on two musical statements, six and nine bars long respectively, each with its own character, scoring and tempo (see ex. 20). These are repeated and extended, sometimes very considerably, five times over and then superimposed before leading to the slow movement. The plan below gives some indication of the proportions of the opening movement:

Statement 1	(A)	6 bars
	(M)	9 bars
2	(A)	9 bars
	(M)	16 bars
3	(A)	23 bars
	(M)	54 bars
4	(A)	46 bars
	(M)	90 bars
5	(A)	96 bars
	(M)	31 bars

Final section (combining (A) and (M)) 67 bars.
Throughout, A and M have separate tempi: Allegro non troppo e pesante ♩ = 88, and allegro molto e con grande energia ♩ = 132, respectively.

ex. 20

Some new thematic material emerges from the extension of the original invention: for instance, a dance-like duet for the violins (starting at fig. 20), whose true significance is not revealed until the final section of the movement. As is clear from the plan above, the 'Arrest' music is allowed fullest scope in the fifth statement, where it, too, can grow in richness and splendour.

The sharp polarities on which the opening movement is founded return as the basis of the final pages of the symphony: they underlie the setting of the last two stanzas of the final song, 'I Have a Dream', and are encapsulated in the sequence of *forte* and *pianissimo* chords with which the work ends (ex. 21).

The slow movement in Part I and the scherzo in Part II offer some respite from the overt conflicts prevalent in the rest of the symphony. The aggressive dialectic of the opening of the work gives way eventually to music that is predominantly static and introspective. Conceived as a kind of 'nature-music', it contrasts high and low textures—'the windless night sky and

119

ex. 21

[sequence repeated]

the tidal wave below' (in the composer's own words)—using two groups of motifs: the first has a tiny sequence of repeated notes on solo viola and a distant fanfare on two oboes as its reference-points (fig. 105); the second grows from a web of ideas for divided lower strings and clarinets (fig. 115). There is no development of these motifs; they meet briefly, that is all. Tippett brings back the viola motif near the end of the work (fig. 284) again to distance the conflict. The scherzo, on the other hand, bustles with high spirits. It is outdoor music after the manner of Ives's *Fourth of July* or *The Housatonic at Stockbridge*. The composer describes it as 'a play of five different musics which are quite long sections that hardly change at all in themselves but do change in their relationship with each other'. The idea is carried over from the cinematic 'dissolves' in

The Knot Garden, though there the components were not so complex in themselves. It entails a fresh conception of orchestral tutti (as in the Concerto for Orchestra), since when everyone plays we hear five different ensembles running independently; they are not intended to blend as in the orchestral tuttis of Brahms. All five 'musics' are lengthy and elaborate. They comprise an extended motif for four horns; a rhythmically free theme for cellos and basses; fast semiquavers for the violins; a fully-scored chordal motif for woodwind; an extended motif for piano. The culminating 'jam-session' here is interrupted by the Beethoven Ninth Symphony quotation, introducing the vocal finale, an extraordinarily abrupt sequence of stylistic shifts (see figs. 174–192).

The device of a vocal finale is partly Tippett's answer to the vexed question of symphonic last movements: once more he avoids late romantic bombast and orchestral rodomontade. Originally, the blues he had in mind were purely instrumental. But, studying Mahler's *Das Lied von der Erde*, he became sure that vocal blues were more appropriate. In Mahler he discerned formal symphonic balances within the layout of the song-movements and he felt that his own vocal settings would not upset the progress of the symphonic argument. Rather, he could make specific the general polarities of toughness and tenderness outlined in instrumental terms earlier in the work.

Tippett's text for the blues crystallized out of his feeling that the ecstatic celebration of the brotherhood of man in Beethoven's Schiller setting can no longer—after two World Wars, the horrors of the concentration camps, Siberian labour camps and Hiroshima—be taken at face value. The modern sensibility unavoidably qualifies its hopes and dreams with an ironic awareness. The blues, a source of therapy as well as an anguished mode of expression, embody this duality. Tippett's four blues, with instrumental breaks and a Miles Davis-inspired flugelhorn obbligato, show a human progress through birth, innocence and experience. Each verbal metaphor looks back to Schiller and ironically contradicts his rejoicing in a future brotherhood of man. Thus, for instance, 'They sang that, when she waved her wings, the goddess Joy would make

121

us one' is given a modern perspective:

> *'And did my brother die of frostbite in the camp?*
> *And was my sister charred to cinders in the oven?*
> *We know not so much joy for so much sorrow.'*

The blues alternate slow-fast-slow-fast and then lead to a direct commentary upon Beethoven/Schiller; the Ninth Symphony quotation appears three times at climactic points, and the thematic polarities of the first movement reappear as the music gathers rhetorical impetus for the final section, evoking Martin Luther King's dream of a more compassionate world. But the opposites remain unresolved, right through to the bleak chordal confrontation which concludes the work (ex. 21 on p. 120).

Tippett's longest and least 'pure' symphonic work has aroused disfavour amongst those who dislike art that preaches a message. But the cohesion of its abstract and dramatic ingredients is one of its most remarkable features. Overall, it moves from the general to the particular and back again with unswerving conviction.

As if to dumbfound his critics, Tippett went on immediately to compose a Third Piano Sonata (1972–73) which stands as a formidable piece of abstract composition. It has no 'impurities', no quotations from Tippett's own or any other composer's music. It balances the most variegated invention against the tautest organizational principles. It is also music that springs organically from the nature of the instrument and performance upon it, involving the virtuosity of two sets of fingers. Tippett was never a fluent pianist, but he understood the instrument's sounds and potential. The pianist Paul Crossley, who commissioned the sonata, helped the composer realize his *Hammerklavier*-like ambitions (especially in the finale) in as practical a form as possible. Tippett himself comments that 'the independence of the hands is explored chiefly in the outer fast movements [of the sonata] and the unity in the slow middle'. In effect, this means an emphasis on linear writing in the outer movements and vertical textures in the central one.

Tippett's reconciliation of sonata-style methods and fantasia procedures here is impressive. The first movement is a sonata-allegro of the kind we find in late Beethoven: compressed, yet a tumult of ideas, mysterious and elevated in style. The thematic material and its development are cunningly fused. First come two starkly opposed musical statements: one consisting of angular two-part highly syncopated dancing counterpoint; the second (beginning after a bar's rest), quiet chords spanning out across the keyboard. Then a smoother version of the opening counterpoint (again giving prominence to the interval of a minor ninth) turns—after being interrupted by some jaunty dotted-rhythm counterpoint—into overt development of the opening idea, absorbing the dotted-rhythm counterpoint in the process. An entirely new motif—chords surrounded by wide-leaping staccato phrases—ushers in all the original material, now decorated throughout with trills. The last four bars of the initial idea are raised by a tone, and the music continues at the higher pitch thereafter, until it is interrupted by the last six bars of the development section now raised by a fifth; the music is then left hanging in the air.

The controlled flux of this sonata reaches an apogee in the central movement, a series of four meditative variations on a sequence of seventeen six-part chords presented decoratively at the start. The impulse towards variation is strong from the outset: hence chord 12 is never heard other than as a pattern of intricate embellishments. The four variations transpose the chords up a minor third each time, so that by the fourth they are back at their initial level. Thus Tippett obtains the most comprehensive range of colour, texture and register from the piano. Even then, he gives the movement a focus by allowing a simple melody to emerge in the third variation. After the repose of this movement, we return to the forceful mood of the first movement, for the finale relies again on angular two-part counterpoint proceeding at high speed, with hardly any respite. The music does reach a momentary rest-point (bars 350–352), but then returns along its previous path: the centre of the movement is thus an exact palindrome of what had gone before. The opening section is recapitulated,

123

but shortened and joined on to a coda where the ruthless rushing semiquavers and violent repeated chords reach their zenith: in sum, a *tour de force* in economy of design and uncompromising directness of statement.

In the three instrumental compositions that have followed upon the composition of Tippett's opera, *The Ice Break*, the trend towards synthesis and a new formal pedigree have become evident. Each of them is in a single movement—a continuous span of music, whose component sections are nevertheless distinguishable. In purely abstract terms, the Fourth Symphony (1977) has a cleverly conceived process of articulation, allowing both sonata and fantasy models to have an impact on the unfolding of the music. On the one hand, there is the main process that resulted in four main sections— roughly corresponding to the Beethovenian exposition, slow movement, scherzo and final recapitulation; then there is another, subsidiary process, indebted to the fantasia, which interpolates episodes of development and thematic jux- taposition. Consequently, the work falls into seven sections, dovetailed to produce an unbroken flow of ideas and argu- ment. Its notional archetype is the symphonic fantasia as exemplified by Sibelius' Seventh Symphony.

Yet there are dramatic ingredients in this symphony, too, relating it to the symphonic poems of Liszt, Strauss and Elgar. In these, as Tippett has observed, the programmatic element is ultimately only an alibi, enabling the composer to produce a concentrated outpouring of music within a continuous, often lengthy and elaborate design. Tippett also links the symphony with the symphonic poem tradition when he describes it as a 'birth-to-death' piece (of Strauss' *Ein Heldenleben*). He refers specifically to an early experience of some relevance to the symphony.

Back in the 1920s, he was taken by friends to the Pitt-Rivers anthropological museum in Dorset. There he saw an early film of a foetus growing inside the womb of a rabbit, with the process speeded up so that, at a particular stage, the initial single-cell form shook like a jelly and became two, then later became four. This birth-image remained in his mind. It underlies certain of the motifs in the Fourth Symphony, and this bears especially upon the central climax (in section 4). A significant role is attached to the wind machine in the score: this relates to the overall theme, with 'gentle breathing' sounds indicated at the start and the whole symphony dying away with this instrument sounding on its own. It could well be argued that the wind-machine is (in Boulez' jargon) too 'anecdotal'. To be sure, Tippett somewhat carelessly allowed the instrument to be named in the score before he had discovered its unsuitability (for it only offers icy blasts suited to a Sinfonia Antartica) and tested out alternatives. Since its première, the composer has stated his preference for either a specially programmed synthesizer or live human breathing amplified by a microphone. Both alternatives have proved useful, though in performance the sounds emitted can turn out to be redolent of a space-fiction film or a bordello.

The scoring of Tippett's Fourth Symphony has its own particular slant, the brass being especially prominent (six horns and two tubas are specified in addition to the normal complement). Thematically, it relies on sharply characterized contrasts between the various instrumental families. After the initial introduction, three main musical ideas are stated—on brass, strings and woodwind, respectively; in the score, these are marked 'power', 'vigour' and 'lyric grace'. This exposition culminates in an outburst dominated by the brass and leading to a poetic six-horn passage, answered with equal sensitivity by woodwind, piano, solo viola and double-bass, to finish on a timpani roll. The subsequent development section—in four easily identifiable stages (starting at figs. 25, 33, 40 and 46)—comes back to this poetic outburst, which this time sounds a tone higher and leads without a pause into the slow movement. Here, Tippett considers from four different angles related musical material: a flute theme taken up by the bassoon and commented upon by the other instruments; a brass motif which introduces a tender theme for lower strings (fig. 62); and an oboe theme (fig. 68 *et seq.*), the most extended in the work, to which the cor anglais provides an epilogue (fig. 75).

Another development section is interpolated: a fugal treatment of a craggy string theme, bringing the symphony to its emotional peak, a climax of great violence, from which we are released into the scherzo (fig. 100). Tippett's writing here is concise, even cryptic, but it allows great virtuosity in the scoring, especially in a trio section for six horns (fig. 112 *et seq.*). After the return of the main scherzo material, the fantasia element comes right to the fore. Tippett takes 36 bars of a Gibbons three-part fantasia (one from which he had, years earlier taken a theme for the first movement of his *Divertimento on Sellinger's Round*) and paraphrases it, keeping to three parts throughout, but elaborating and enriching the lines (fig. 129). This pendant to the scherzo reaches again the musical outburst that closed the exposition, again transposed up another tone.

Now Tippett begins to 'collect up' his motifs, in a manner recalling the closing pages of his Second Piano Sonata. This brings us to the last section, where the opening exposition is recapitulated, but modified to feature some spacious contrasts between the different groups of instruments and ultimately to die away to nothing. These last recollections, in which all previous experiences flash by as if in a moment, are the most difficult to realize in performance. But they are integral to a work in which, generally, the aims and techniques cohere remarkably well.

Tippett's String Quartet No. 4 (1978–79) and the Concerto for Violin, Viola and Orchestra (1979) both explore further the possibilities of one-movement form. Although neither has a specific programme or even a suggestion of one, like the Fourth Symphony both encompass a whole cycle of experience in much the same manner as Beethoven's late works. From this sequence of compositions, there also emerges a new strain of lyricism. In the symphony, it takes its place alongside other elements, remaining part of a judiciously balanced scheme. In the quartet, it all but displaces the other ingredients: and in the concerto it is simply predominant throughout, what little tension or conflict there is being relegated to incidental or background status. Tippett has moved sharply away from the hard-hitting, compact style of *The Ice Break* and earlier works.

He has not thereby succumbed to mere nostalgia for the Eden of *The Midsummer Marriage*, for his harmonic language retains too great an asperity for that. His ability to let his music sing again so radiantly is hard won, and all the more impressive as a result.

The quartet and the concerto both begin—like the symphony—with a kind of 'birth' motif although the path each work will take thereafter is quite different. With the quartet, the motif bears particularly upon the slow movement, setting in train a succession of ardent thematic ideas that become the emotional apex of the work. These consist of duets for the two violins and the viola and cello, respectively; a cello solo decorated by the two violins and (at its close) the viola; gently murmured exchanges between viola and second violin against a chordal background, developing into full blooded rhetoric; and a lengthy final episode where each instrument wings along its independent course, before being interrupted by the strife of the finale.

Around this slow movement, the other sections group themselves to show what the composer called 'the general progression (repeated) . . . from a web of sound unwinding into linear clarity, and from intense stillness breaking out through the unwinding into vigour'. This progression is encapsulated in the opening slow movement, whose function is largely introductory, producing for us the germ cells of all the later motifs. Conflict then comes clearly to the fore in the second movement. The musical material here—three contrasting themes, with linking ideas and an extended codetta—is heard three times over, transposed and presented in a slightly different order at each repetition.

Tippett also extends and develops some of the material, producing an elaborate texture of counterpoint that brings the musical tension to a peak. Respite from this only arrives with the main slow movement. As in the earlier string quartets, Tippett's style seems steeped in imagery derived from late Beethoven; for instance, in the linking of the introductory section with the second movement, a feature adopted from Beethoven's String Quartet in E flat major, Op. 127 (ex. 22).

127

ex. 22

Beethoven

Tippett

No. 2

The Beethovenian reference point becomes quite overt in the finale of Tippett's quartet. After an opening eruption of violence, the music focuses on a theme whose dotted rhythm inescapably recalls the fugue subject of Beethoven's *Grosse Fugue* (ex. 23). Its treatment is equally obsessive, though not fugal.

Rather, Tippett is intent on taking us towards clarity and this is apparent from the linking episodes of fast semiquavers. At the opposite extreme from the main dotted-rhythm motif is a chordal theme based entirely on harmonics. The two are polarized against each other for some time, before the earlier eruption of violence returns and gives way suddenly to a slow coda which gently leads us into the quietude of the final bars—a final transformation of the chordal motif present in different forms throughout the work.

The coda modifies marginally any impression we might have that this quartet, like the Fourth Symphony, is another birth-to-death piece. Overall, this description would fit: the music of the quartet burgeons from stillness into effortful existence, as does the symphony; both works also embrace conflict, dreams and passions, ending in the stillness of death, all passion spent. But the sudden descent into a peaceful rapture amid the conflict of the finale of the quartet, suggests the possibility of a new beginning: and this beginning is indeed the *raison d'être* of the Triple Concerto. In the coda to the quartet, all four instruments are able to sing together yet maintain independence of line. From the start of the concerto, the three soloists are introduced (viola, cello then violin) as separate musical personalities, then they join together to play music that is explicitly based upon the coda of the quartet (ex. 24, p. 131).

Tippett's Triple Concerto deserves the title *'Fantasia Concertante'* even more than Tippett's earlier Corelli-based work, bearing that name. For its formal shape stems primarily from the nature of its invention. Out of the elaborate patchwork of sections in the first of its three movements, there emerges an overall binary scheme, in which the five main musical components introduced at the start are re-aligned, modified or transformed. We should observe immediately that its opening 'birth' (or maybe 'creation') motif introduces each part, transposed up a tone on its second appearance. The main focus is, of course, the lyricism of the solo writing. The other ingredients provide only a context for this. When, after two orchestral episodes, the soloists start to play again (fig. 16), it is as if their earlier colloquy had only been adjourned. In the second part of the movement, there is one new idea (fig. 52) enabling the solo violin to give a fresh perspective to the argument.

Linking the three movements are short interludes of 'non-music' after the manner of the 'dissolves' in *The Knot Garden*. The first (fig. 67) is evocative in character, relying on the gentlest sonorities of tuned percussion, harp and horns— entirely apposite as preparation for the perfumed paradise garden that comprises the slow movement. The second interlude features timpani and untuned percussion and its fanfare-like outbursts on the brass serve to galvanize the music afresh for the finale.

The slow movement shows plenty of evidence of Tippett's response to Javanese music, which he heard in the flesh for the first time not long before he began the concerto. Intuitively he has absorbed and emulated those textures in gamelan music wherein a solo singer, perhaps also a flute or (bowed) string instrument join together for the same serene flow of endless melody. Surrounding the melody are the gentlest of gong sounds which (to Tippett's ears) add a bluesy colouring to the inflexions of the melody.

Formally, this movement is quite straightforward with two orchestral episodes (figs. 96 and 103) temporarily halting the flood of decorative lines from the soloists. Tippett embellishes even further the ornate solo lines, by giving two of the soloists an obbligato orchestral instrument. The cello (fig. 85 *et seq.*) pairs off with the bass oboe; the violin (fig. 98 *et seq.*) is partnered by an alto flute. Moreover, at the point where the violin and viola embark on a duet in canon (fig. 105 *et seq.*), there is an obbligato of fast pizzicati from the orchestral strings. In the slow movement, all tensions are pushed into the background. There is an interesting analogy here with Nadia's death scene in *The Ice Break*. Brass fanfares that previously occupied much of the foreground of the action are now distant recollected images.

In the finale of the concerto, the orchestra presents the main thematic ideas—after a slow introductory section featuring each soloist in turn—and then the soloists extend and embellish these in their separate ways. Lyricism now overtakes the orchestral texture, as the violins, violas and cellos enunciate a tune with an Elgarian gait which the composer marks 'singing, rich and golden', the brass providing punctuation. This tune unfolds further in three stages, after the soloists (at figs. 127 & 130) have added their own commentary (see figs. 130 & 133). Then Tippett begins to 'collect up the pieces', as it were, just as he did in the Fourth Symphony and, much earlier, in the Second Piano Sonata. The fast theme of the first movement is recalled (fig. 138) and after the soloists have supplied a dancing counter-theme, we reach once more the 'birth' motif and the soloists' original cadenzas, modified somewhat. Our final impression of the work has to centre upon the generous, superabundant melody that comes from the soloists. This is emphasized by the return of the original colloquy (see ex. 24) from the first movement, now projected even more ardently.

That there should be an orchestral pendant to this simply to close the work, seems to matter very little: the music has already pressed home its regenerative message.

Tippett's synthesis of formal and stylistic elements in these last three compositions—the Fourth Symphony, Fourth Quartet and Triple Concerto—betokens a technical mastery which has been achieved with much effort. Such mastery serves its own ends within these works, but it is also a firm basis for the composer's most ambitious projects. In this sense, we can also regard the symphony, the quartet and the concerto as preparation for Tippett's next major work embodying a theme of some dimensions: the choral and orchestral work, provisionally entitled *The Mask of Time*, which he started early in 1980 and which he hopes to finish in 1983 or early 1984. Its theme is of a visionary cast—Man and Time. Significantly, it already quotes the opening of the Fourth Symphony.

8 TIME AND ETERNITY

A VISIONARY ELEMENT IS unmistakable in the music of Michael Tippett. He is aware of it himself. He speaks of music being a 'significant image of the inner flow of life'. Taking into account the special awareness which he possesses, he can define (in a memorable passage) his own role as an artist thus: '. . . I know that my true function within a society which embraces all of us, is to continue an age-old tradition, fundamental to our civilization, which goes back into prehistory and will go forward into the unknown future. This tradition is to create images from the depth of the imagination and to give them form, whether visual, intellectual or musical. For it is only through images that the inner world communicates at all. Images of the past, shapes of the future. Images of vigour for a decadent period, images of calm for one too violent. Images of reconciliation for worlds torn by division. And in an age of mediocrity and shattered dreams, images of abounding, generous, exuberant beauty.'[54]

Tippett, then, is a composer prepared to stretch himself well beyond his known capacities. His music often moves into territory so unusual as to defy easy analysis or conventional description. One of the earliest examples of this is the fourth movement of his Third String Quartet. No precedent exists for its formal shape. No expressive model from any past music underlies its progress from complete stillness to a passionate discharge of lyricism. It is not fanciful to see in it a musical

134

metaphor for the act of creation itself. Only someone with Tippett's daring and visionary certainty could have produced it.

The same high aspiration informs the whole of *The Midsummer Marriage*. Tippett's concept of the stage as 'one of depth'—as one that embraces worlds 'within or behind the world of the stage set'—ensures that it can be the medium for a searching study of the human psyche, reaching a climax in Madame Sosostris' aria in Act III. Tippett reveals himself in this character and in the other Messenger-figures Hermes and Astron, in *King Priam* and *The Ice Break*. Madame Sosostris' aria, and the hymn to 'divine music', sung by Hermes in the final interlude of *King Priam*, were both inspired by Paul Valéry's poem, *La Pythie* (1918). This poem is similarly concerned with 'the quest for a poetic language, the evolution of a cry into ordered discourse'.[55] Hermes' aria—which, Tippett has said, 'speaks for me'—comes to its focus in a Yeats quotation: 'Mirror upon mirror, mirror is all the show'. It gives the cue for Priam's final vision, as he awaits death. Priam has come to a 'loop in time', and, his eyes closed to the external world, he murmurs:

> *'I see mirrors*
> *Myriad upon myriad moving*
> *The dark forms of creation.'*

In *The Ice Break*, Astron—a somewhat androgynous figure from the supernatural world, after the example of Balzac's Seraphitus-Seraphita—brings the opera to its intended climax of revelation in the scene entitled *The Psychedelic Trip*. Unfortunately, this scene does not live up to its aims. The flow of lyricism characteristic of Tippett's music in all such visionary episodes is subverted by the restless tempo and fragmented outline of the music. One cannot help feeling that it should be less inhibited. The 'storm in the universe' experienced by the chorus of seekers might have been tumultuous. Against it, Astron's ironic self-debunking

135

ought to be breathtaking. Yet it hardly registers. The scene is one of Tippett's few failures in a domain where normally he enjoys prodigious success.

Tippett's visionary powers stem from an acute sense of the independence of the creative faculty from external and even internal ferment: a wilful concentration of psychic energy towards specific and extraordinary goals. Tippett pinpoints this notion in an essay commenting upon Edgar Wind's 1960 Reith Lectures, *Art and Anarchy*.[56] Here he arrives at a stage where he confesses himself 'haunted by the feeling that creative time may really be spontaneous and discontinuous'. The comment is apposite in relation to the music of the fourth movement of his Third String Quartet and the operatic scenes just mentioned. In each case the emphasis is on a sense of endless inventive flow in the musical ideas and apparent freedom from formal restraints.

Tippett develops this notion most fully and explicitly in *The Vision of St. Augustine* (1963/5). Close scrutiny of this work reveals a tautly held design. But its temporal discontinuity and apparent spontaneity of utterance upturn all one's formal expectations. Tippett's mosaic-style fantasy procedures are now at the service of an almost 'stream-of-consciousness' manipulation of a text drawn from St. Augustine's *Confessions* and other Biblical sources.

It would be easy to take this composition at face value and find in it an explicitly Christian mysticism. Yet its theme is more specific: man's capacity—or incapacity—for transcendent experience. Augustine provided the stepping stone. Tippett had read in an essay by Gilles Quispel[57] how Augustine had introduced a new idea about time into Christian thinking: God is present not only in the cosmos but in man's innermost soul. Time, being a 'working' of God, acquires a psychological nuance. The present is nothing if not an experience in the soul; the past is a memory image in the soul; and the future exists only as our psychic expectations. Ordinary time is transient and meaningless. It disappears when the soul unites with God. 'Divine time'—or Eternity—is thus separable from measured worldly time. The soul shifts so speedily from the present (*contuitus*) towards the future (*expectatio*) or the past (*memoria*) that it is forever distended (*distentus*) in all directions without a centre. To achieve a centre, concentration (*intentio*) is necessary. Augustine's two visions gave him an intimation of such a centre.

Tippett concentrates upon the second of Augustine's two visions, setting the famous sections of Book XI of the *Confessions*, wherein Augustine describes the vision of eternity he shared with his mother, Monica, whilst standing in a window embrasure. But Part I of the work contains a remembrance also of the first (auditory) vision—shared with Augustine's friend Alypius—of a child singing. Indeed, immediately in Part I, we meet the procedures that are characteristic of the entire piece. The narrative entrusted to a solo baritone—setting the scene in the house where Augustine and his mother were resting before their sea journey back to Africa—is interrupted and illuminated by the chorus, with reminiscences of other experiences, hymns, prayers and exclamations.

Individual words sung by the baritone bring associative choral interjections into play. '*Tu*'—referring to Monica— prompts a recollection of the Ambrosian hymn, *Deus, Creator Omnium*, which the grief-stricken Augustine had repeated to himself at his mother's death (ex. 25). '*Ipsa*' sparks off a recollection of both parents. '*Fenestram*' ('window') is echoed in a great choral shout, and '*unde hortus*' ('whence the garden') takes us towards Augustine's first vision. All the strands so far encountered are collated as we reach the climax of Part I, the vision itself: worldly time yields to eternity, which is the life of the saints and which is made manifest in the paeans of joy sung by the angels. The chorus now supplements Augustine's semi-articulate description with poetic rhapsody from the Book of Job (*'Ubi eras quando ponebam fundamentam terrae?'*) and Psalm 42 (*'Quaemodum desiderat cervus'*): but it is the orchestra which alone enables one to meditate fully upon the vision and the experience that has accumulated in connection with it.

ex. 25

To attain an effective relationship between baritone and chorus and to transmit musically the range of interrelated feelings implicit in the text, Tippett develops further in this work his mosaic-style methods of construction. In the work as a whole, there are 14 thematic blocks, each designated a tempo. Seven of these are introduced in Part I. Moreover, the first two—four bars of baritone solo accompanied by lower strings, piano and percussion, followed by 12 bars of choral commentary, with a similar accompaniment, but with an important celesta motif as decoration—engender many of the other thematic ideas in the piece (see ex. 26). Exposition and development overlap throughout: hence the fluidity of cross-

ex. 26

reference and the apparent spontaneity that arrest and hold the listener's attention.

In general, the musical material transforms itself into dance-like mutations which are the final ecstatic goal. For instance, the baritone's opening phrases (especially the second) become more rhythmically alive in the chorus part at '*Surge, surge acquile*' (fig. 23), generate an imitative dance for xylophone and piano at '*abcessi ergo*' (fig. 28), and another lively version at the baritone and chorus exchanges beginning '*et praeterita*' (fig. 43), which leads eventually to the leaping motifs that embody the choral 'alleulias' (fig. 61 *et seq.*) and the long orchestral coda into which they develop (fig. 68). Likewise, the opening phrases of the chorus acquire new rhythmic interest at '*et inspira*' (fig. 13), and in conjunction with the xylophone/piano duet at '*abcessi ergo*' (fig. 28). At '*et praeterita*' (fig. 43), they issue in a new accompanimental motif on violins and violas. Thus Tippett manages to ensure both formal cohesion and relevance to the unfolding of the text, no matter how intricate its layout.

A similar progression towards an ecstasy given a dance-like expression is evident in Tippett's vocal writing. The dancing melismas present in all Tippett's vocal music, from his early cantata *Boyhood's End* right up to *King Priam* (in Achilles' war-cry), are now elaborated into what the composer calls *glossolalia*, an ancient tradition of exultant wordless vocalization. *Alleluia*, *jubilus*, yodelling, the singing of any number of jazz and rock-artists—these share in that tradition. Augustine himself tells of the *jubilus*. 'For those who sing in the harvest field, or vineyard, or in work deeply occupying the attention, when they are overcome with joy at the words to the song, being filled with such exultation, the words fail to express their emotion, so, leaving the syllables of words, they drop into vowel sounds—the vowel sounds signifying that the heart is yearning to express what the tongue cannot utter.'

The *glossolalia* in *The Vision of St. Augustine* coincide with temporal shifts and with the concentration that produces a meditative focus or centre. We meet this vocal technique as the basses sing the *Deus, Creator Omnium* (see ex. 25, p. 138) for the first time in Part I. Against this line, the female voices sing ecstatic culminative melismas, and the baritone ululates on the word '*Tu*' which provokes both a memory—a temporal shift—and a concentration of psychic energy in the chorus part. '*Fenestram*' and '*unde hortus*' later (fig. 19) have a similar effect. Just as the thematic material evolves into dance-formats, so the vocal lines strive towards exultant '*alleluias*'. In his previous composition, the Concerto for Orchestra (1962), Tippett explored the possibility of 'non-ends'. Here, he puts the technique to more deliberate use, in deploying a mosaic of fast-changing patterns (fig. 68 *et seq.*) which could continue for ever. From two bars of invertible counterpoint and a single-line answering phrase one bar long, together with a trumpet theme, Tippett draws a series of oscillating, whirling per-mutations which twice reach a momentary point of rest, but whose capacity for further extension is limitless (ex. 27). Eternity is, so to speak, written into the musical design at this point.

Although in Parts II and III of the work, seven blocks of thematic material at different tempi are introduced, the sense of continuity from all that has preceded it is unbroken. In Part

ex. 27

II, Tippett is dealing with the more important of Augustine's two visions. 'We passed through the various levels of bodily things, and the sky itself, whence sun and moon and stars shine upon the earth. And higher still we soared thinking inwardly and speaking and marvelling at your works; so we came to our own souls and went beyond them, so that we might touch that region of unending richness whence you feed Israel forever with the food of truth . . .'

This striving towards the inner vision, this light in the soul is Tippett's main preoccupation now. The texture he creates owes much to the example of the slow movement of his Concerto for Orchestra, moving with an agonizing effort from the very low to the very high. The baritone line itself echoes the viola melody that emerged in that slow movement (see figs. 84–87 in the Concerto and figs. 90–93 in *Vision*). Tippett supplements Augustine's text first with three other instances of inner illumination, as experienced by the blind Tobias, and by Isaac and Jacob, who both lost their sight in old age. In all three episodes of analogy the chorus is barely articulate. The lower voices can only utter the inceptive *'O lux'* ('O light') in a stuttering rhythm; the female voices get stuck in the middle of their sentences and a solo soprano has to carry the burden of the text apprehending the vision.

The musical texture elaborates steadily into an extra-ordinary sonority of five-part lower strings, three-part male voices, two-part female voices, soprano solo and baritone solo, piano, tamtam, bass drum, bass-clarinet, bassoon and contra-bassoon. Its main upward impetus comes from the solo voices and the insistence of sopranos and altos upon a motif derived from their earliest musical material in Part I. The climax occurs at the point where the baritone sings *'et venimus in mentes nostras'* ('and so we came to our own souls') and the female voices of the chorus join in with *'intravi in intima mea, et vidi lucem incommutabilem'* ('I went into myself and saw the unchangeable light'). Here the violins take over the stuttering rhythm of the lower voices, and a tiny trumpet obbligato, clarinet and cymbal rolls surround the voices with a celestial aura. The vision is shared. The chorus, outside it all, as it were, comments, *'O*

142

aeterna veritas et vera caritas et cara aeternitas!' ('O eternal truth and true love and beloved eternity!')—all sung in octaves and unisons. Augustine's vision promotes an identification with God and specifically His powers of temporal transcendence. Thus with a blaze of fanfares and choral exclamations the visions of Parts I and II are brought together. The dance-rhythms return, the chorus refers back to the bass solo (*'et praeterita'*) they accompanied in Part I (cf. fig. 43 and fig. 124), the *'alleluias'* become resplendent, once more prompted by the same quotation from Psalm 42 as appeared in Part I. But Augustine's vision is ultimately a personal one; the chorus must stand outside it to some extent, repeating in awe the phrase *'o aeterna veritas'*. In the closing pages of Part II, Tippett recapitulates the opening, taking over into the orchestra some of the ideas previously allotted to or shared with the chorus— muted trumpets now have the little phrase sung previously by female voices (cf. fig. 144 and fig. 91); horns take over the *pulsando* stuttering of the tenors and basses. Two new elements are added: an ascending phrase for three horns, and solo flute and clarinet lines. These, in a way, symbolize the en-raptured state of Augustine's mind in the moment of vision.

Part III of the work presents us with a large conditional clause. *If* the world, *if* heaven, *if* the soul itself, *if* our own breathing, our own voices could fall silent, could be still, then would we not experience the eternity that is the life of the saints? Life would cease to be the usual sequence of antici-pation, then fleeting, momentary insights followed by a loss of vision and mere recollection. Instead, the present would become in its entirety revelation and life itself eternal.

Whereas the focal image in Part II was that of light, at the start of Part III, it is silence. The chorus constantly echoes the baritone with the word *'sileant'*. As in the Second Piano Sonata and Concerto for Orchestra, Tippett fragments and collects together the pieces of his musical mosaic: here, he does so specifically in order to incorporate recollections of the vision of Part II. The movement effectively synthesizes all the material of the work. It brings back the *Deus, Creator Omnium*, it repeats the climax of Part II.

143

Augustine's mystical victory is once more celebrated. Music that appeared in both the earlier parts—at *'et praeterita'* in Part I and in Part II (cf. figs. 43 and 124)—reappears in Part II at *'sicut nunc extendimus nos'* ('and reaching for these things that are before all time', cf. fig. 189). The *'alleluias'* this time culminate in Augustine's final cry, *'Intra in gaudium domini?'* ('Enter into the joy of your lord?')—'gaudium' producing an exultant melisma accompanied by dancing figurations on the piano and xylophone, along with woodwind. The chorus caps this cry with a massive choral outburst *'Attolite portas'* ('Lift up your heads, O ye gates'), from Psalm 24. The image is apposite. The 'everlasting doors' of the text evoke the 'window' through which earlier Augustine and his mother had perceived their vision.

But there is now a postscript. A hush descends. The chorus, first singing in Greek, then whispering in the vernacular appropriate to the place of performance, mutter words from St. Paul's Epistle to the Philippians: 'I count not myself to have apprehended.' Augustine himself has previously quoted much from St. Paul, especially the half-sentence, 'and forgetting the things that are before' (i.e. the things before time, before the creation of the world). But Augustine omits 'I count not myself to have apprehended'. St. Paul humbles himself before the mystic experience, so does Tippett—and so do we, at the composer's instigation. Psychologically it is very sharp. We are not saints. We cannot count upon a future perception of eternity. Probably it will be denied us.

In Tippett's career, *The Vision of St. Augustine* is one of the peaks. Not since *The Midsummer Marriage* had he unleashed such a torrent of musical invention; nor had he held to a single theme with such unremitting fervour as we find here. The work will always seem exceptional, because it is difficult to perform. Its choral writing taxes the most skilled professional singers; and only the most dedicated and impassioned interpreter can reproduce both its clarity and its ardour. But maybe its very isolation will be a source of strength. One could not easily bear a plethora of performances: for the work burns too deeply.

144

9 PORTRAIT OF THE ARTIST

TIPPETT HAS ALWAYS implicitly accepted the Frazer-derived notion of a primal, worldwide religion of mankind, characterized by certain archetypal events and expressed in tribal societies through vegetation magic. Francis Cornford's theories—also Frazer-derived—about the origins of tragedy and comedy in ancient Greece, led him to the format for *The Midsummer Marriage*. So, in the opera, we find the traditional *agon*, or combat between the seasons, along with the death of the year-king or year-god: and, of course, fertility is once more perpetuated.

From all this comes the emphasis in Tippett's work as a whole upon human reconciliation and renewal, even when it is clear that conflict will be resumed at some future date, to be resolved all over again. 'The moving waters renew the earth', sing the soloists and chorus in the final General Ensemble of *A Child of Our Time;*

> *'Spring, spring*
> *Spring come to you at the farthest.*
> *In the very end of harvest'*

declares the chorus whirling through the hospital in the penultimate scene of *The Ice Break*. In the music of Tippett's later years—since 1965 or so—this prospect of hope and forgiveness has become a precarious feature. For Tippett has

145

become closely identified with the ironic sensibility which (following John Fussell)[58] he recognizes as endemic to the civilized world since the First World War. He was never able to produce mere 'pie-in-the-sky' expressions of optimism; and his compassion waxes no less strongly than in his younger days. But now the dream of the peaceable kingdom is harder to sustain.

Hence we have the self-debunking of Astron in *The Ice Break*

> *'Saviour?! Hero?! Me?!!*
> *You must be joking!'*

All the hope Astron can offer is

> *'Take care for the earth.*
> *God will take care for himself.'*

(a quotation from Jung).

Tippett's Third Symphony touches one raw nerve after another. The climax of its bitterness is

> *'My sibling is the torturer;'*

and again

> *'We fractured men*
> *Surmise a deeper mercy;*
> *That no god has shown.'*

The conclusion of this work shows us the conflict between Tippett's desperate desire for a compassionate world and his ironic awareness of the brutality of the age. Although he can say with Luther King, 'I have a dream', he knows that the promise will be broken, over and over again. Thus, in the music for this declaration of faith in humanity, we find no sense of the 'spontaneous and discontinuous' as elsewhere in his work. The polarities that have rent the music asunder since the inception of the symphony remain.

146

In *The Vision of St. Augustine* Tippett seems to suggest that the highest role for the artist is to act as a kind of shaman, as an envoy between this world and the world of the spirit, drawing us by sheer intensity into an ecstatic trance-like state. At the same time, he has never been able to shut himself off from the world. His work remains human—all too deeply human.

The closest self-portrait he acknowledges is that contained in the character of Dov, the musician in *The Knot Garden*, whose subsequent spiritual development is charted in *Songs for Dov* (1972). Dov sings not only for himself, but for all his generation. Because he is a musician he is a divided man: he has to recognize a tug-of-war between expressing his own situation, and making impersonal utterances of relevance to us all. This psychological duality is reinforced by Dov's sexual ambivalence. In the last scene of Act II of *The Knot Garden*, he is able to show compassion and tenderness towards the disturbed adolescent Flora. But then he sings his own song directly to the audience. This is repeated as the first of the three songs that comprise *Songs for Dov*. Dov's howls of anguish—standing for the general human condition of loss and heartbreak—uttered against the music heralding his arrival on stage with Mel in Act I, Scene IX of the opera, precede the first two songs here.

Dov travels round the world as both loner and musician, 'searching for that southern land where we hope never to grow old, but which, proving an illusion, drives us ever on towards another beckoning country; a singer, then, who sings of the *Wanderjahre*, those years of illusion and disillusion, innocence and experience, which we all pass through to reach what maturity we may; and then journeying "full circle west", back to the "big town" and the "home without a garden" across the tundra of Siberia. Dov, as the grown man, the fully-fledged mature creative artist, struggles with the intractable problems of "poets in a barren age" . . . '[59]

Here we reach a theme that has always been close to Tippett's heart: the tension between the pastoral and the urban, between the eternal values of nature and the ephemera of the town. Tippett, through Dov, joins Pasternak (who spoke through Zhivago) in suggesting that the lyric poets of the

147

present day could try and sustain the pastoral metaphor against the changing fashions of the town. Whereas 'the living language of our time is urban', there are, however, no poems which exemplify it. Pasternak can only produce rhetoric:

> 'Then why does the horizon weep in mist
> And the dung smell bitter?
> Surely it is my calling
> To see that the distances should not lose heart
> And that beyond the limits of the town
> The earth should not feel lonely?'

Dov, searching within himself for something more poetic, can for the moment only discover two words—which Tippett divides with a tap on the claves:

> 'Sure, baby.'

The verbal and musical imagery of *Songs for Dov* both play upon the divisions within Dov's personality and the cultural dichotomy he experiences in the world at large. The first song—structurally the simplest, in verse and chorus form—brings pulsating electric guitar rhythms and bluesy melodic inflexions into the foreground. It should be remembered that in its operatic context it was a direct response to Flora's ostensibly backward-looking song, taken straight out of Schubert's *Die schöne Müllerin*. The second and third songs become more complex, as a consequence of the collage techniques which Tippett applies to both words and music.

Each of the three verses of the second song (after its howling introduction) starts with literary and musical quotations. These signify the choice of roles the artist can assume: escapist; exponent of ritual; slavish upholder of ancient traditions or neo-classicist. Dov ultimately rejects them all. The first line of Mignon's song from Goethe's *Wilhelm Meister*, 'Kennst du das Land' and the two quotations from Beethoven's setting of the poem are counterpoised against musical phrases invented by Tippett himself, at the start of the first verse (ex. 28). The second song begins with similar juxtapositions, using this time Tippett's own setting of Ariel's song in *The Tempest*, 'Come unto these yellow sands' as its reference-point. For the third verse, Tippett has the opening line of the sirens' song in Homer's *Odyssey*, set to music that originated in *King Priam* (the final scene of Act I—fig. 179—where Paris responds to Helen's seductive invitation), and this again is answered by Tippett's own individual phrases. The second song as a whole takes Dov through his *Wanderjahre*. He travels to Mignon's 'land of flowering lemons', to Ariel's 'island with the gold-sand beaches'. From the 'canting sirens', 'banging on dead men's bones', however, he steals only a song which he wants for his own purposes as a musician. He then begins the return journey home.

The three chorus sections in the second song represent Dov's outward journeying and signal his eventual turn around. Each is compounded of minute quotations and references interspersed and combined with percussive repeated patterns. We hear the whistle of the 'iron horse' or train; the whirring wings of Pegasus, the flying horse; the horns quote Wagner's *Flying Dutchman*; the strings and percussion recall the gallop of the 'live horse' in filmed westerns:

ex. 28

150

> 'Ride off into the sunset
> I'm on my way.'

The second song leads straight into the third by way of a piece of 'dissolve' music: music first heard in Act I of *The Knot Garden*, (fig. 14), introducing Thea, whose romantic horn-motif and high shimmering strings acquire a new plangent oboe solo at the start here. The song is through-composed. Dov now faces his final choice of roles as creator. He can be a purveyor of messages to mankind; a rhetorician. Or he can sing from the heart: a lyricist. The division within himself on this issue affects all mature artists. Dov, coming back 'full circle west', back to the 'big town' across the tundra of Siberia, goes to look in on Zhivago and Lara in the 'forest hut where they had shacked up together'. He finds only a fragment of a love poem, for the two lovers have

> 'gone away
> Back to the town . . .
> Each, alone, into the swarming city.'

For this Siberian journey, Tippett develops mainly the two Thea motifs introduced at the opening of the song, but it incorporates a tiny quotation on the viola from Moussorgsky's opera *Boris Godunov*. The tenderness of the poetic fragment is also encapsulated in a quotation of the music with which Dov cradles Flora in her distress at the end of Act II of *The Knot Garden* (fig. 94). But we are intended more to focus on the way the music moves through a series of stylistic leaps and bounds to its apogee. 'The living language of our time' sparks off two episodes of Tippettian boogie-woogie. Ultimately we reach the rhetoric of the final Pasternak setting ('Then why does the horizon weep' etc.), where stark wind chords and a wailing trumpet melody are answered antiphonally by string phrases. The ironic conclusion—'Sure, baby'—seems but the beginning—if there could ever be one—of a new set of songs.

Taken as a whole, we can see that Dov's journey to maturity as an artist leaves behind his initial innocence (Song I); rejects

151

in turn neo-classicism, escape into pure self-indulgence, and outmoded ritual (Song II); and considers finally the public art of rhetoric, only to reject that also in favour of a more intimate form of artistic expression. As such, the song cycle can be seen as paradigm of Tippett's own artistic development: for he is now very much at the stage where rhetoric has given way to lyricism.

The element of collage in this work, taken overall, has much in common with the strained imagery of the metaphysical poets. There is a similar sense of worlds and of temperaments in sharp collision. The seventeenth-century metaphysicals, such as John Donne, Andrew Marvell or Abraham Cowley, drew together the definitions and distinctions of medieval scholasticism, the new ideas in emergent science and in systematic materialist thinking, along with a fresh curiosity about the psychology of love and religion, to fuse them all into fantastic verbal conceits.[60] Likewise Tippett, throughout his career, and especially in his compositions of the 1970s, has charged his work with every conceivable experience, from the arts and the sciences, from the I-Ching to bio-genetics. Hence his fondness for collage—an overt means to show an interaction of metaphors far removed from each other. If there is a specifically English tradition to which he relates, it is certainly to Shakespeare and the Metaphysicals, whose efforts to synthesize disparate ideas and experiences, ancient and modern, he seems to emulate. Furthermore, in Tippett's view, the Pilgrim Fathers took with them much of this Shakespearean culture when they went to the USA. The collision there in modern times of many traditions and cultures would seem to him only a further extension of that pluralist Shakespearean world. Hence his tendency to regard himself as an Anglo-American figure rather than a British one.

During his fifty years or so as a composer, Tippett has undoubtedly cultivated a distinctive language of his own. The prime emphasis in this language has been on a linear organization of musical ideas, helped by a genuine flair for colour and texture, and his propensity for using a variety of formal processes to interact with each other. Balanced against the rigour with which he has exploited these facets of his style is the freedom with which he treats harmony.

Broadly speaking, there are two phases in his work as far as harmony and tonality are concerned. Early on in his maturity he openly defended the classic tonal system,[61] and always used it, if freely. This freedom led him, in *King Priam*, to move decisively away from a traditional use of tonality. Ever since, he has thought more deliberately about the vertical aspect of music, inventing empirically the harmonies he needs for particular musical or dramatic contexts. He has arrived at a very flexible notion of 'expanded tonality' in the process. The nearest we can come to describing this notion in detail is to say that he regards all the semitones within the octave as having enharmonic equivalents, thus giving him a 24-note scale from which he can build any number of contrasting harmonic colours. This approach persists in his music right up to the present, for it serves his image-making role as a creative artist. Sometimes it results in a musical 'fingerprint' that is instantly identifiable: e.g. Tippett's favourite way of symbolizing sensual rapture is through the use of chords built upon fourths and centred around A flat major (cf., the line 'In the meadows of her breath ...' in *Compassion* from *The Heart's Assurance*; the final section of Sosostris' aria in Act III of *The Midsummer Marriage*; the opening of the Piano Concerto; and the second thematic group of the first movement of the Second Symphony).

But it should be stressed that no harmonic system as such emerges from his work. Likewise, Tippett's modification of sonata-style presentation to allow his most unexpected flights of thematic inspiration their true role did not result in flimsy musical construction. With equal individuality he developed his own methods of attaining cohesion within the design of each work. Sometimes these come close to twelve-note method (as in *The Knot Garden*). But we should not, therefore, read into his harmonic and formal procedures a systematic practice—of one kind or another—which they do not exemplify. Tippett has never accepted *post facto* membership of this school or that coterie, and would certainly turn down an honorary Doctorate in Dodecaphony. He remains ready to utilize any techniques that suit his purpose. But his most recognizable trait remains his melody. This seems to incorporate every other facet of his musical make-up: rhythmic exuberance, harmonic colour, formal diversity. It is capable of taking wing in every expressive context—from the most unaffected and homespun to the loftiest and most passionate. Everything he has written, from First String Quartet to the Triple Concerto, bears witness to this.

For his sheer creative independence and integrity, Tippett is now revered by younger generation composers as diverse as Henze and Berio, Birtwistle, Edward Cowie, Brian Ferneyhough and Robin Holloway. While he has nurtured his artistic skills for their own sake, Tippett has never lost sight of those values that have drawn from him his most committed music. His humanism has a personal basis. The traumas of his childhood and youth loom large. But he can step outside them and relate to world issues on their own terms. He is aware that individuals need to live out their lives to the full. He would still dream of the (imagined?) warmth of the (working-class?) family being a microcosm for harmony in the world at large. He feels that our awareness of the global context of human experience—both in space and time—may modify, though not diminish or invalidate, our ideals and aspirations. We are but specks in the universe: our personal consciousness may be only part of a collective unconscious or destiny that mysteriously shapes our ends.

But the composer has in all this to continue to try to produce music of enduring significance. He owes this to his fellow men. If not a utopian, Tippett remains a tough yet tender idealist and one we should cherish, for such figures are rare enough in any age, let alone our own cruel epoch.

TIPPETT IN INTERVIEW

The contents of this section of the book are based in part on the author's interviews with Tippett and also with Murray Schafer's in *British Composers in Interview* (London, 1963); and upon the E. William Doty lectures in Fine Arts given by the composer at the College of Fine Arts, University of Texas at Austin in 1976 and subsequently published by the University Press in 1979. The section on Shostakovich is reprinted from Tippett's review of Shostakovich's *Testimony*, published in the magazine *Quarto*, (No. 3, February 1980, p. 7).

Question: *How many hours a day do you compose?*

Tippett: Four. In addition, I used to spend a few hours copying from pencil score to ink score. Recently, however, I have tended to work straight into ink score, using abbreviations which copyists can interpret when producing a neatly written version. That way I can actually compose more!

How much work gets written at an average sitting?

A few bars, sometimes an entire page.

Do you revise your past works ever?

No. Sometimes conductors will make cuts in the operas, but I leave that to their professional discretion. I myself insist on rigorous advance planning of works so that few revisions are necessary.

What do you do when you are not composing?

I read, walk in the fields near my home and plan other works. In the evenings I generally watch television.

The French novelist Simenon said: 'I need to work with my hands. I

155

would like to carve my novels in wood.' To what extent do you feel composing is a physical business?

I like to think of composing as a physical business. I compose at the piano and like to feel involved in my work with my hands, but I wouldn't say putting my hands on the keyboard means as much to me as it might to, say, Stravinsky who, being a good pianist, probably felt composing was something of a fingertip operation. What is certainly clear to me is that I need to make actual sounds, even if they are imperfect and never identical with the sounds of the composition in performance. But with this general aura of sound I make with my voice and the piano, I produce what appears to me quite clearly a physical atmosphere and within this physical atmosphere my creative process is at its strongest—I mean the critical part of the creative process is at its strongest. The inception of creation may be quite apart from anything physical whatsoever.

Is it possible to describe this 'inception of creation'?

I feel a need to give an image to an ineffable experience of my inner life. I feel the inner life as something that is essentially fluid in consistency. The process, which may be rapid or slow, is one of giving articulation to this fluid experience, and appears in successive stages. I begin by first becoming aware of the overall length of the work, then of how it will divide itself into sections (or movements), and then of the kind of texture or instruments that will perform it. I prefer not to look for the actual notes of the composition until this process has gone as far as possible. Finally the notes appear and, in general, I find that during the purely mental process of articulating my imagination, the precise material has been forming itself subconsciously, so that I never have to struggle to find it.

You write your own libretti for your operatic and choral works. Is this because of the poverty of good librettists or is there a deeper reason?

At first that was accidental. I didn't wish to write the libretto for *A Child of Our Time*, it was to have been written by T. S. Eliot. I think I would go so far as to say that with the success of *A Child of Our Time*, which has a simple libretto, I was led to believe that I could do more along this line than I was ready for; and in composing the libretto for *The Midsummer Marriage* I took perhaps too many liberties. I am not certain about this. When I came to compose the libretto for *King Priam*, I certainly did not feel that it needed to be composed by myself; but again on the advice of several people, including Eliot and Christopher Fry, we all came to the conclusion that I should try, with other people's help, to prepare it myself again. And that is the way I have continued ever since.

Do you compose the entire libretto before beginning the composition?

No. What became quite clear was that you must have a deeper understanding of what the musical structure is going to be before you write the entire libretto.

Do you immediately divide your libretti in the classical way into arias, recitatives, etc.?

The libretto for *The Midsummer Marriage* was written in a kind of free verse, and there the scheme on the whole was the scheme of eighteenth-century opera. It did have ensembles and arias and recitative of a kind, though not as dry and defined as in eighteenth-century operas. In *King Priam*, the distinction between the arias and the recitative is less apparent and, on the whole, it is a series of dramatic monologues. There are fewer ensembles and no strophic or *da capo* arias. This seems to suit the character of the work. *The Knot Garden* and *The Ice Break* are different again. In *The Knot Garden*, for instance, there are very few arias indeed. For the middle act, I needed a series of confrontations which were technically duets. I had to work these out first—who met whom, who sang to whom, and in fact before I ever got to the music I guessed what kind of music it would be.

When you quote something in the text, such as 'I had a dream' (in the Third Symphony), or when in King Priam *the chorus suddenly has a line from Dylan Thomas—'The force that through the green fuse drives the flower'—are you using it the way that somebody does in speaking? Are you just borrowing someone else's phrase because it expresses what you want to say particularly well? Or do you want the listener to find*

157

embedded in your text and in your music an allusion to a whole piece of poetry: something that will include that work in yours?

I'd say it's the former. You see, 'The force that through the green fuse drives the flower' comes at the moment in *King Priam* when the Nurse, Young Guard and Old Man (in Act I) are speaking of love; the love which, in the end, produced the destruction of Troy. Very few people know that quotation is there in *King Priam*. If you're not a literary person and you write your own text, you have to be willing to take things from a variety of sources whenever the underlying concept is traditional and everlasting. The spirituals in *A Child of Our Time* are another example. I cannot invent the metaphor in the verbal sense so I have to borrow. Everything can be borrowed in this fashion. With the Third Symphony text, I was deliberately alluding to Martin Luther King, though the fact of there being an allusion is of no consequence. For, of course, we're going to dream and like Martin Luther King we know that what we dream won't come to fruition tomorrow.

On the evidence of your writings, you are very well read. How far have your extra-musical explorations affected your work?

When I was a student, it was commonly felt in England that the composer, and the musician in general, was a person of sensibility, but not of intellect; and, having divided those things artificially, that the conceptual world was something that should not be too obvious in the life of a creative musician—indeed, it was felt unseemly for it to become at all prominent. The notion behind this was, I think, that the metaphor of music was unreal in some way and disrelated to what one might consider a system of thought. By contrast, creative artists in the fields of literature or drama were allowed to use all the intellectual faculties at their command and even be exploratory in a world context. This was certainly the prevalent tendency of that period—the end of the 1920s and early 1930s. Even a great figure like Beethoven was not exempt. In the history books he is made to seem an idiosyncratic non-intellectual. Goethe, by contrast, was practically made out to be the opposite. For him to write a treatise on the theory of colours (not a very good

158

one), and argue with Newton, or go out and find what he called the *Ur-Pflanze*, the plant that he supposed to be the genetic basis of plant life—all this was regarded as reasonable enough, because mental activity of this kind could be, as it were, incorporated within the metaphors of Goethe's literary works.

For myself, there may indeed be two worlds, one subjective and connected specifically with creativity, the other conceptual and concerned with outside things. But they are both in my body. One may be in my head and the other in my stomach, but they're both inside the same organism! I may move into one more than the other at a particular time. In what I call the world of discursive thought I try to analyse and epitomize certain things by means of a conceptual language: but that is not poetic language. When I compose a piece of poetry or compose a piece of music, then I am operating in an entirely different way in a different field. To say what that field is, is very difficult. There are often intellectual concepts within that field that may, as Shakespeare put it, '. . . suffer a sea-change/Into something rich and strange.' That quotation just about sums it up. Yeats described the process by the metaphor of dipping your hand into the great memory: not only your own memory, but the archetypal memory, and producing from this a set of metaphors which you hammer into verse. Such was his method. The actual reason for any particular metaphor may have long antecedents. The process of transformation inside the psyche may be, in fact, no shorter for the poet than it is with the musician. But it is always difficult to say about most music whether the external stimulus—if such exists—is immediate or not.

To what extent do you feel that your originality as a composer is tempered by the awareness of cultural pressures around you, if at all? Are you concerned with whether something is going to be widely performed and accepted? Is that ever a consideration when you're writing a new work?

No, it isn't a consideration, not in the short term planning of a new work. I've always been preoccupied with social pressures, but not necessarily cultural pressures. In a work like *A Child of*

Our Time, directness of communication was an important consideration. Now when it came to *The Vision of St. Augustine*, that could never be so. There is thus in my life a sharp polarity between works. Some, because of their density and complexity have removed themselves from the sphere of direct communication. There are others in which I return to it.

Have you not at some time felt it necessary to break—as some composers have—with tradition? To 'cut out the umbilical cord', as Boulez once put it?

The reference to the umbilical cord was very much used by composers like Boulez who were about 20 when the last war ended. They were part of a syndrome of experience which was also there at the end of the previous World War—which I regard as a climacteric of the age and an even more important turning-point, historically speaking. The breakdown of values in the heartlands of Christian Europe during the First World War was so extreme that you had the appearance of a syndrome called Dada. Dada said that the values that were apparent in, say, music from Beethoven through to Mahler had proved false in every sense—artistically, politically, ethically. An artist of the period must consequently make it all a laughing-stock. I can remember it happening in London. André Breton, one of the foremost Dada figures, arrived to give an example of what art should be by lecturing shut up in a diving-suit. The trouble was that they couldn't open the top and they had to call the fire department to release him!

I am not in a diving-suit. And Dada was a short-lived affair. But it was the springtime of my life—whether it was a false or real spring—and there were other more vital artistic expressions of it—for example the Bauhaus and Diaghilev ballet company. So Dada was swept away. Now it returns again in 1945 with the new generation, in a new form, of course. They said there was no past. We must start again. As Boulez himself once said to me, 'We have nothing.' It didn't directly affect me, though it does in that over my shoulder I realize that there are people like Shostakovich and I remember what *he* lived through. I was living in a society which gave me virtually what

I wanted and didn't threaten to chop my head off. Nevertheless, all this didn't dislocate or divert my own creative development. After all, what did I write immediately after the Second World War? I produced *The Midsummer Marriage*, a life-giving work of great radiance. How could that be of relevance to a world which had just dropped the atom bomb on Hiroshima and which had only lately opened the concentration camps? *The Midsummer Marriage* was simply written in an extreme polarity to the cultural and social pressures of its period. That is something which seems to be fundamental to me as an artist.

You have often spoken of your indebtedness to Beethoven, Purcell and certain other figures. But you generally mention Shostakovich only in passing. Are you disturbed by this composer? How do you view him—morally, politically, as well as artistically? Has your view of him been altered or affected by the recently published memoirs of Shostakovich? Did you ever meet him?

Shostakovich's *Testimony*[62] was addressed to his countrymen, not the West—which is Shostakovich's name for Europe and America. He was a slavophile not a Westerner. He disliked the West intensely and he seems concerned in this book to make certain truths known to a future generation of Soviet composers. In order to do this he felt that he must send his manuscript illegally to the West, so that after his death—since the manuscript, if discovered in Russia might have been destroyed—it could be 'returned' for a kind of 'publication'. The mechanism is that the Russian version of the manuscript would be beamed back to Russia by radio and there picked up and transcribed by devoted listeners who type it on to *samizdad*. It's a method which in principle has been used in Russia since Tolstoy. It was even for security purposes used by Krushchev.

The process may seem strange, but it is natural enough in dealing with any form of censorship. In my student days, for example, the two major literary works banned in England by the censors were Joyce's *Ulysses* and D. H. Lawrence's *Lady Chatterley's Lover*. The manuscripts of these were sent to France for publication and then brought back in printed form to

161

England illegally: that is how my generation read them. The difference with Russia would seem to be only a matter of degree. Nevertheless, it is surely pusillanimous for a major state like Russia to be unwilling to allow publication of *Doctor Zhivago*, which has already been read by everyone who wishes to read it in *samizdad*. *Testimony* is being read in Russia in this way already.

I had two 'non-meetings' with Shostakovich. The first would have taken place in 1949. This was a period when, after the war, the Communist powers were attempting a series of international conferences on peace. There had been one in Warsaw and there was to be a more spectacular one in New York. It was announced that Shostakovich was to be present in New York and he himself in *Testimony* gives an account of his appearance there.

I was surprised to receive an official invitation to this conference since, as a Trotskyite, I had been debarred previously from all contact with the Stalinist faithful. Nevertheless, it seems to have been felt that, since I had been sent to prison as a pacifist, my dilettante Trotskyism could be safety overlooked. Some ex-Trotsky friends attempted to persuade me that I should go to New York in order to ask Shostakovich questions concerning the notorious 1948 decree of Zhdanov on the Arts. This would have made Shostakovich appear a political coward in the most public manner possible. I refused. I explained that if I went to New York at all I should try to ask questions which would show Shostakovich that I understood the meaning of Siberia. This was regarded as strange at the time since all the present disillusionment in left-wing circles with the Communist regime had not begun. It was probably easier for me, both because of my Trotskyist affiliations and pacifist convictions. Thus I always knew that both Hitler and Stalin were monsters, though one was the enemy and the other was the ally.

In New York Shostakovich was in fact asked the questions. With his head down he answered them all as Stalin had ordered. Shostakovich describes his experience in New York:

People sometimes say that it must have been an interesting

trip, look at the way I'm smiling in the photographs. That was the smile of a condemned man. I felt like a dead man. I answered all the idiotic questions in a daze, and thought, when I get back it's over for me.[63]

The moral question as to what answers he was expected to give comes in the book in the generally elliptical manner in which he speaks of these things. He speaks through another person. The most moving and personal account is in his description of Meyerhold's last theatrical production:

Just before the Theatre of Meyerhold was shut down, Kaganovich [a Communist party leader and brother-in-law to Stalin] came to a performance at the Theatre. He was very powerful. The Theatre's future depended on his opinion, as did Meyerhold's future.

As was to be expected, Kaganovich didn't like the play. Stalin's faithful comrade-in-arms left almost in the middle. Meyerhold, who was in his sixties then, ran out into the street after Kaganovich. Kaganovich and his retinue got into a car and drove off. Meyerhold ran after the car, he ran until he fell. I would not have wanted to see Meyerhold like that.[64]

It is quite clear that people of Shostakovich's integrity were unaware of what they were doing and I am certain that the constant necessity to act in this manner within Russia itself agonized him to the very end. He made this crystal clear, in his elliptical manner, by a similar story concerning Akhmatova, the marvellous poet who, a generation older than Shostakovich, had such great courage. Her poet-husband Gumilyov was shot quite early on in the purges and her son was taken to Siberia. Stalin demanded that she should write a 'celebratory' ode in his honour if she wished him [her son] to live. Akhmatova and Zoschenko, a satirist and playwright, and close friend of Shostakovich, were forced to meet a delegation of tourists:

... The old trick, to prove that they were alive, healthy and happy with everything, and extremely grateful to the Party and the government.

163

The 'friends' with meal vouchers in their hands couldn't think of anything cleverer to ask than what Zoschenko and Akhmatova thought of the resolution of the Central Committee of the Party and Comrade Zhdanov's speech. This is the speech in which Akhmatova and Zoschenko were used as examples. Zhdanov said that Zoschenko was an unprincipled and conscienceless literary hooligan, and that he had a rotten and decayed socio-political and literary mug. Not face; he said mug.

And Zhdanov said that Akhmatova was poisoning the consciousness of Soviet youth with the rotten and putrid spirit of her poetry. So how could they have felt about the resolution and speech? Isn't that sadistic—to ask about it? It's like asking a man into whose face a hooligan has just spat, 'How do you feel about having spit on your face? Do you like it?' But there was more. They asked it in the presence of the hooligan and bandit who did the spitting, knowing full well that they would leave and the victim would have to stay and deal with the bandit.

Akhmatova rose and said that she considered both Comrade Zhdanov's speech and the resolution to be absolutely correct. Of course, she did the right thing, that was the only way to behave with those shameless heartless strangers. What could she have said? That she thinks she's living in a lunatic asylum of a country? That she despises and hates Zhdanov and Stalin? Yes, she could have said that, but then no one would have ever seen her again.

The 'friends' of course could have bragged about the sensation back at home, 'among friends' . . . And we would have all suffered a loss, we would have lived without Akhmatova and her incomparable late poetry . . .[65]

(I would like to say that I have total sympathy with Akhmatova and by implication with Shostakovich. It is also clear that I would never have had probably more than one-fifth of Akhmatova's courage.)

Has the book changed my view of Russia or of Shostakovich? *Testimony* tells us nothing new about the general condition of Soviet intellectual life before and after the

164

war—nothing that one might not have gathered from, say, the two volumes of memoirs by the widow of Mandelstaum, or those of Galina von Meck. Some circumstantial details are, of course, different and only serve to accentuate the fact of its being written for Shostakovich's countrymen, who would know all the numerous subsidiary figures of whom he speaks. Neither does the book change my limited understanding of Shostakovich, though it certainly fleshes out my previous guesses.

Some of one's intimations of the truth have come always from the music itself. To give a personal example: I first heard Shostakovich's Eleventh Symphony only about four or five years ago. This symphony is supposed to be concerned with the events of the 1905 revolution. I was quite sure when I heard it that the use of 1905 was a kind of political alibi, since this was a matter of known revolutionary history. The music to me was self-evidently about Shostakovich's own experiences in the continual catastrophe of his life. This he confirms:

> I wanted to show this recurrence in the Eleventh Symphony. I wrote it in 1957 and it deals with contemporary themes even though it's called 1905. It's about the people, who have stopped believing because the cup of evil has run over.[66]

What is new to me is his categoric statement that he knew this to be entirely understood by his public. The music must remain his only true memorial, and this because it is a music which, carrying the message of humanity under stress, has crossed all frontiers to speak to the world, though experienced by a composer of a dedicated patriotism.

My second 'non-meeting' was in 1968, in the autumn following the invasion of Czechoslovakia. I was rung up by someone at the Russian Embassy in London to ask whether I would agree to go as guest of honour to the Moscow meeting of the Congress of Soviet Composers. Once again I refused; partly because I was very busy at my own composition but also from some instinct. The Congress, of course, took place. Kosygin and Brezhnev were present at the opening plenum (according to the account in *The Times*). Shostakovich began the whole affair by reading a special resolution of thanks to the Red Army for their heroic deeds. Presumably he might once more have asked us to comprehend, by reference to Akhmatova. Yet it must appear strange that he would still feel that way since Stalin was dead, the thaw had taken place, and he had an impregnable position in Russian society. Could he not have refused? The explanation lies in his deep agony of spirit between his love of Russia and her great history and his experience of its present corruption (his own word). Like Solzhenitsyn a generation later, he felt a duty to write the truth down for the generation to come. But when Solzhenitsyn asked him to sign some public protest, he refused. He was moving towards his death, profoundly embittered; and at least according to his editor, Solomon Volkov, he felt himself out of touch, even rejected by the very young composers. So we must comprehend.

I am glad I did not go to Moscow. I would not have wanted to see him like that.

Every composer, painter, sculptor, architect in the twentieth century has to deal with a detachment from tradition—be they traditional beliefs or whatever. What would you suggest for people who are trying to construct a kind of do-it-yourself epistemology for their art? For instance, a Christian artist would start with the basic belief that God existed, God was there. An existentialist would say that God was not there.

My epistemology is an endless agnosticism. It must be because I could not put it down any other way.

As I understand it, when Dante wanted to have an epistemological basis, he could read St. Thomas Aquinas and take the Thomist philosophy as something absolutely real to him. We're in a position now where we tend to reject the whole lot. Do-it-yourself? I very much doubt that epistemology can ever be construed as a do-it-yourself kit, but I think it must have some relation to a collective moment in history. So the answer is that somehow one has to manage without that certainty. When I speak to the Hindu or the Buddhist, I only do so by moving outside epistemology and trying to find some

166

rather incoherent kind of humanism. I believe it is fundamentally an incoherent force and could never be any different.

A few years back, I received a copy of the latest issue of *Index* magazine containing all sorts of literature that had been censored. There was in this a set of short poems by a young Polish poet which had been censored in this way, but were now translated and made available. Amongst them was one tiny poem which was concerned with what the poem could do as a tiny voice in this great world. It was addressed to me, to you, to himself, to God.

One of the lines which went right inside me was: 'Cherish the man, but do not choose the nation.' That's me, too. It gives me courage, for it seemed to me a signal. I suggest that if he heard *A Child of Our Time* he, too, would get a signal. But I'm sure that if he and I tried to get together and form a party or collective or even an epistemology, we should merely deceive ourselves.

NOTES

The following abbreviations have been adopted in notes references:

MAI   *Moving into Aquarius* Michael Tippett (Paladin, 1974)
MAII   *Music of the Angels: Essays and Sketchbooks of Michael Tippett* Ed. Meirion Bowen (Eulenberg, 1980)
SB   *Michael Tippett: A Symposium on his Sixtieth Birthday* Ed. Ian Kemp (Faber, 1965)
AMT   *Michael Tippett: A Man of Our Time* Catalogue of the Tippett Exhibition (Schott, 1977)

Chapter one

1   *Musical Composition: A Short Treatise for Students* Charles Stanford (London, 1911) Ch. 2, p. 10.
2   MAI, p. 152.
3   MAII, pp. 117–126.
4   cf. AMT, pp. 40–53.
5   HMV DA 19/21–2.
6   In 1962, Hartog left Schott's to run the leading concert agency, Ingpen and Williams; Tippett is one of the artists he represents.
7   cf. MAII, pp. 77–84.
8   Paul Sacher (b. 1906) founder/conductor of the Basle Chamber Orchestra and of the Schola Cantorum Basiliensis. His name is celebrated for the remarkable list of compositions he commissioned from major composers (such as Bartok and Stravinsky) and for the help he gave to musicians in distress in the pre-war and wartime periods. Tippett visited him often in the Fifties to conduct the Basle Orchestra and enjoy some much needed holiday.
9   Cecil Smith in the *Daily Express* 28 January 1955.

Chapter two

10 '...In music, practicability of text may not be the concern of the critics: to orchestral players in the mass it may mean the difference between confidence and doubt. The comprehensive technique of the BBC Symphony Orchestra is equal to all reasonable demands.' R. J. F. Howgill, BBC Controller of Music, in *The Times* 21 February 1958.

Chapter three

11 cf. below pp. 123–4.
12 cf. below pp. 145–52.

Chapter four

13 cf. MAII pp. 117–26.
14 cf. SB pp. 47–9.

Chapter five

15 MAII, pp. 127–87.
16 ibid., p. 193.
17 ibid., pp. 193–6.
18 ibid., pp. 121–3.
19 ibid., p. 119.
20 ibid., pp. 138–9.
21 cf. Sir Michael Tippett (Phonogram brochure, 1975).
22 'Music and Poetry' in *Recorded Sound* No. 17, Jan. 1965, pp. 287–8.

Chapter six

23 MAI, p. 50.
24 ibid., pp. 54–5.
25 ibid., p. 58.
26 ibid., p. 53.
27 ibid., p. 56.
28 cf. Tippett's letter to Eric Walter White 14 September 1949. 'In a biography of Saint Joan I read yesterday the historical material for the couplet 'Joan heard the voice first/In father's garden at high noon'. *Tippett and his Operas* Eric Walter White (Barrie & Jenkins, 1979, p. 58). The biography to which Tippett refers is *The Saint and the Devil: A Biographical Study of Joan of Arc and Gilles de Rais* Frances Wimwar (Hamish Hamilton, 1948).

29	*Lapis Lazuli.*
30	cf. Tippett's letter: 'I've come across some fascinating allied stuff in a Yeats biography (Norman Jeffares). Yeats equates the four elements to four (historical) ages. (I'll show you his notes to the poem.)

> He with body waged a fight
> Body won and walks upright.   (Earth)
>
> Then he struggled with the heart;
> Innocence and peace depart.   (Water)
>
> Then he struggled with the mind;
> His proud heart he left behind.   (Air)
>
> Now his wars with God begin;
> At stroke of midnight God shall win.   (Fire)

It's the last couplet that's interesting—and Yeats's (similar) order.' White, op. cit., p. 58.

31	cf. White, op. cit., pp. 55 ff.
32	cf. MAII pp. 222–3.
33	*The Hidden God*, Philip Thody's translation of Goldmann's *Le Dieu Caché* (Routledge, 1964), p. 333.
34	'Music and Poetry' in *Recorded Sound*, No. 17, Jan. 1965, p. 290.
35	MAII, p. 230.
36	'Music and Poetry', op. cit., p. 291.
37	MAII, p. 231.
38	cf. Sir Michael Tippett (Phonogram brochure, 1975), p. 11.
39	References to this poem also occur in Tippett's sketches for *The Midsummer Marriage*: its central image has been an abiding preoccupation.
40	In the Covent Garden and Kiel productions, he was a rock superstar, while in Boston he was a boxer.
41	It is, in fact, a transformation of the scene in Shaw's *Back to Methuselah* in which the egg with a girl inside appears on stage: she asks to be let out, the egg is cracked open and she goes straight for the first handsome man she sees. Lev's reference to the 'naked human chick' here preserves the original image. cf. Michael Tippett, *Back to Methuselah* and *The Ice Break* in the *Shaw Review*, Vol. XXI no. 2, May 1978, pp. 100–3.
42	MAII, pp. 52–5; 208.

Chapter seven

43	MAI, p. 101.
44	Sleevenote for Philips recording.
45	William Glock (b. 1908) was then music critic for the *Observer*. A

pupil of the pianist Artur Schnabel, he was later to have a distinguished period as both performer and administrator, most notably as BBC Controller of Music (1959–72) and as director of the summer schools at Bryanston and Dartington Hall. In 1974, he succeeded Tippett as Artistic Director of the Bath Festival.

46   The *Observer*, 25 April 1943, reprinted in AMT, p. 36.

47   cf. *Rhythm in Tippett's Early Music* Ian Kemp (Proc. of the Royal Music Association, Vol. 105, 1978–9) pp. 142–53.

48   cf. below p. 134–5.

49   *The Orchestral Composer's Point of View* Ed. Robert S. Hines (University of Oklahoma, 1970) p. 209.

50   cf. Hines, op. cit., pp. 210–1.

51   cf. SB pp. 176–9; also Hines, op. cit., pp. 211–9.

52   Hines, op. cit., p. 204.

53   cf. *How Does it Feel?* Ed. Mick Csaky (Thames and Hudson, 1979) pp. 173–80 (an essay by Tippett on the genesis of the Third Symphony).

Chapter eight

54   MAI, p. 156.

55   *Poems* Paul Valéry (Collected Works, Vol. 1, Routledge & Kegan Paul 1971, translated by David Paul) note on p. 459.

56   cf. MAII, pp. 37–43.

57   *Time and History in Patristic Christianity* in *Man and Time: Papers from the Eranos Yearbooks* Ed. Joseph Campbell (Routledge & Kegan Paul, 1958) Vol. 3, pp. 85–107.

Chapter nine

58   '...There seems to be one dominating form of modern understanding: that it is essentially ironic; and that it originates largely in the application of mind and memory to the events of the Great War.' *The First World War and Modern Memory* John Fussell (Oxford University Press, 1975) p. 35.

59   MAII, pp. 236–8.

60   cf. *Metaphysical Lyrics and Poems of the Seventeenth Century* Ed. Herbert J. C. Grierson (Oxford University Press, 1921) pp. xiii–lvii.

61   cf. MAII, pp. 31–3.

Tippett in Interview

62   *Testimony: The Memoirs of Dmitri Shostakovich* Ed. Solomon Volkov, translated by Antonia W. Bouis (Hamish Hamilton, 1979).

63   ibid., p. 152.

64   ibid., p. 60.

65   ibid., p. 156.

66   ibid., p. 5.

GLOSSARY OF TECHNICAL TERMS

aria: a defined composition for solo voice; usually it has an instrumental accompaniment and the vocal part itself is quite elaborate. The aria figures prominently in seventeenth and eighteenth-century cantatas and oratorios and in opera, where it has a clear function as a dramatic soliloquy providing release from the onward flow of the action; as such it contrasts completely with **recitative** (see below).

blues: a type of black American popular music, flourishing in the twentieth century, and quite separate from jazz in its history and evolution. A characteristic of both vocal and instrumental blues is an expressive flattening of the third, seventh and (to a lesser extent) fifth degrees of the scale (known as 'blues notes' when this happens).

cantata: a composition for one or more voices with instrumental accompaniment. Usually it consists of a number of movements (e.g. arias, duets, **recitatives** etc.) which are based on a continuous narrative text. It is the most important and ubiquitous type of vocal composition in Europe in the seventeenth and eighteenth centuries.

chromatic: the use of pitches not present in the **diatonic** scale (see below) but resulting from the sub-division of a whole tone into semitonal intervals. The application of this principle to all five whole tones of the diatonic scale produces the chromatic scale with twelve notes to the octave. *Chromaticism* in music arises from a melodic and/or harmonic emphasis on the chromatic scale.

counterpoint: a term denoting music in which two or more independent vocal or instrumental lines are sounding simultaneously.

continuo: in eighteenth-century music, the continuo is the part improvised from a given bass to supply richness and rhythmic vitality with the texture of instrumental or orchestral ensemble.

diatonic: music making use of the notes of the scale consisting of five whole tones and two semitones.

divisi: literally *divided*; a term used to indicate that an instrumental body (e.g. cellos or violins) might be divided into two or more groups for the

172

execution of certain passages involving more than one line or a chord-sequence.

dodecaphony: a term used as a synonym for 12-note or serial technique.

fantasia: in general this refers to a kind of composition in which 'flights of fancy' or sheer invention takes precedent over conventional formal procedures.

fugue: the most ordered form of music with a contrapuntal texture.

gamelan: the generic name for an Indonesian orchestra consisting of gongs and other percussion instruments.

ground bass: a bass line with a distinctive pattern which is repeated over and over again with varying music for the upper parts. The *ground* belongs to the general category in music of continuous variations (see also **passacaglia**).

madrigal: name given to two different types of vocal music, one of the fourteenth century in Italy, the other of the sixteenth century, flourishing especially in Italy and England. At its most typical, it entails vocal writing in four to six parts, a style generally polyphonic and imitative, and an expressiveness that is closely allied to the text in both meaning and punctuation.

melisma: a group of more than five notes sung to a single syllable. The term tends to be applied universally, but has been most used with reference to medieval western music, especially religious chants.

obbligato: means 'obligatory' or 'necessary'; it usually refers to an independent part in ensemble music, ranking in importance just below the principal melodic line and not to be omitted.

oratorio: a composition with an extended libretto, usually of a religious or contemplative character, that is performed in a concert hall or church without scenery, costumes, or stage-action. Solo voices, chorus and orchestra take part, but the chorus has the prime role.

ostinato: a clearly defined phrase which is repeated persistently, most often in immediate succession, throughout a composition or a section of a composition.

passacaglia: originally a dance-form, it issues in the seventeenth century in Europe as a composition consisting of continuous variations on a clearly distinguishable repeated pattern (or **ground bass**).

recitative: a style of vocal setting intended to imitate and emphasize the natural inflexions of speech. It entails a purely syllabic treatment of the text, speechlike reiterations of the same note, slight melodic inflexions etc. Its function in opera and oratorio is to carry the action forward from one aria (or ensemble or chorus) to the next.

scherzo and trio: a movement in a sonata or symphony or quartet (rarely in a concerto) which was introduced by Beethoven to replace the conventional minuet and trio. Its distinguishable features are a rapid tempo in 3/4 metre, vigorous rhythms and unpredictable elements, sometimes of a humorous or ironic character. The trio section is the middle episode which alternates (sometimes more than once) with the main scherzo-music, usually involving a contrast of orchestration in symphonic works.

serial technique : an extension of the variation technique evolved by Schoenberg involving the use of a 12-note theme as the basis of a composition; serialism also implies a choice of rhythms, timbres, etc. as a basis for variations in a piece.

sonata-allegro (*sonata-style allegro*) : this refers to the formal plan adopted in the opening movements—and sometimes slow movements and finales—of solo instrumental sonatas, symphonies, quartets etc. in the late eighteenth and nineteenth centuries. It entails an argument centred on two or three thematic groups (though sometimes single themes are made to serve the purpose, simply changing their character as and when necessary) and a planned sequence of key-modulations beginning and ending at the same point.

song-form : simple ternary form ABA—a form actually more common in instrumental music than songs.

through-composed : a translation of the German term, *durchkomponiert*, applied to songs in which new music is provided for each stanza of the text, thus ensuring a strongly felt dramatic or narrative continuity (cf. Schubert's *Der Erlkönig*). The term has also been used in the context of opera, where a composer has not set his libretto as a sequence of separate recitatives and arias, but as a continuous flow of music such as in Wagner.

tremolo : in music for stringed instruments, the fast reiteration of the same note produced by rapid up-and-down movements of the bow.

(More thorough and detailed examination of terms used in the Glossary can be found in such reference-books as the *Harvard Dictionary of Music*, Ed. Willi Apel, the *New Grove Dictionary of Music and Musicians*, Ed. Stanley Sadie, and *The Oxford Companion to Music*, Ed. Percy Scholes.)

SELECT BIBLIOGRAPHY

The most complete and up-to-date bibliography, listing all Tippett's compositions and recordings of them, Tippett's prose and verse writings, and all published writings about Tippett and his music has been compiled by Paul D. Andrews. This was published by Bedfordshire County Library, with addenda, in 1980. The following selection is indebted to Andrews's bibliography. Further acknowledgement is due to the catalogue of the composer's works published by Schott & Co., and the lists compiled by Alan Woolgar for the exhibition catalogue *A Man of Our Time* and his Tippett discography in *Records and Recording*, February 1980.

Writings by Michael Tippett

The most important of Tippett's prose and verse writings are contained in two volumes:

Michael Tippett: *Moving Into Aquarius* (Routledge & Kegan Paul, 1959; Paladin, 1974, containing extra material)

Meirion Bowen (ed.): *Music of the Angels—Essays and Sketchbooks of Michael Tippett* (Eulenburg, 1980)

Writings about Tippett

Clements, Andrew: *The Ice Break* (*Music and Musicians*, Vol. 26, No. 1, September 1977, pp. 42–4)

——. *Tippett's Fourth* (*Music and Musicians*, Vol. 27, No. 1, September 1978, pp. 20–22)

Crossley, Paul: *Tippett's New Sonata* (*The Listener*, Vol. 89, No. 2304, 24 May 1973, p. 697; reprinted in *Tippett's Piano Sonatas*, Schott, 1975)

Dickinson, A. E. F.: *Round About the Midsummer Marriage* (*Music and Letters*, Vol. 37, No. 1, January 1956, pp. 50–60)

——. *The Garden Labyrinth* (*The Music Review*, Vol. 25, No. 11, July 1971, pp. 176–80)

Fingleton, David: *The Ice Break* (*Music and Musicians*, Vol. 25, No. 11, July 1977, pp. 28–30)

Jacobson, Bernard: Essay in *Tippett in America* (Schott, 1975)

Kemp, Ian: *Michael Tippett—A Symposium on his Sixtieth Birthday* (Faber, 1965)

——. *The Dream Works of Tippett* (*Times Literary Supplement*, 27 October 1972, pp. 1275–6)

——. Article in *The New Grove* (Macmillan 1981, Vol. 19, pp. 1–11.)

Mason, Colin: *Michael Tippett* (*Musical Times*, Vol. 87, No. 1239, May 1946, pp. 137–41)

——. *Tippett and his Oratorio* (*The Listener*, Vol. 38, No. 972, 11 September 1947, p. 452)

——. *Michael Tippett's Opera* (*The Listener*, Vol. 53, No. 1439, 20 January 1955, p. 129)

——. *Tippett's Piano Concerto* (*The Score*, No. 16, June 1956, pp. 63–8)

——. *Michael Tippett's Piano Concerto* (*The Listener*, Vol. 56, No. 1439, 25 October 1956, p. 681)

——. *Cobbett's Cyclopaedic Survey of Chamber Music, Vol. 3* (OUP, 2nd edition 1963, pp. 99–103)

Matthews, David: *Michael Tippett—An Introductory Study* (Faber, 1980)

Mellers, Wilfred: *Tippett and his Piano Concerto* (*The Listener*, Vol. 61, No. 1554, 8 January 1959, p. 80)

——. *Michael Tippett and the String Quartet* (*The Listener*, Vol. 66, No. 1694, 14 September 1961, p. 405)

Milner, Anthony: *Rhythmic Techniques in the Music of Michael Tippett* (*Musical Times*, Vol. 95, No. 1339, September 1954, pp. 468–70)

——. *The Music of Michael Tippett* (*Musical Quarterly*, Vol. 50, No. 4, October 1964, pp. 423–38)

Northcott, Bryan: *Tippett Today* (*Music and Musicians*, Vol. 19, No. 3, November 1970, pp. 34–5, 38, 40, 42–5)

——. *Tippett's Third Symphony* (*Music and Musicians*, Vol. 20, No. 10, June 1972 pp. 30–32)

Porter, Andrew: *The Ice Break* (*The New Yorker*, 19 September 1977; reprinted in *About the House*, Vol. 5, No. 4, Christmas 1977, pp. 48–50)

Rubbra, Edmund: *The Vision of St. Augustine* (*The Listener*, Vol. 75, No. 1920, 13 January 1966, p. 74)

Schafer, Murray: *British Composers in Interview* (Faber, 1963, pp. 92–102)

Souster, Tim: *Michael Tippett's Vision* (*Musical Times*, Vol. 107, No. 1475, January 1966, pp. 20–22)

Spence, Keith: *Midsummer Marriage and its Critics—A Topical Retrospect* (*Musical Times*, Vol. 112, No. 1535, January 1971, p. 28)

Sutcliffe, Tom: *Tippett and the Knot Garden* (*Music and Musicians*, Vol. 19, No. 4, December 1970, pp. 52–4)

Warrack, John: *The Vision of St. Augustine* (*Musical Times*, Vol. 107, No. 1477, March 1966, pp. 228–9)

——. *The Ice Break* (*Musical Times*, Vol. 118, No. 1613, July 1977, pp. 553–6)
White, Eric Walter: *Michael Tippett and his Operas* (Barrie & Jenkins, 1979)
Whittall, Arnold: *Music since the First World War* (OUP, 1977, pp. 212–34)
——. *Britten and Tippett: Studies in Themes and Techniques* (OUP, 1982).
Michael Tippett: A Man of Our Time (Catalogue of the Tippett Exhibition, Schott, 1977)

CHRONOLOGICAL LIST OF COMPOSITIONS

Most of Tippett's compositions exist in two manuscript versions: a preliminary pencil score and a 'final' copy in ink.
* Manuscript in British Library
† Manuscript in BBC
** Manuscripts in British Library and private collections
†† Manuscript at Barber Institute, University of Birmingham
*** Manuscripts at British Library and Library of Congress
††† Manuscript in Private collection
**** Manuscripts in British Library and Northwestern University, Illinois, USA

Early Works

(Unpublished, by the composer's own decision)

c. 1928   String Quartet in F minor

1928–30   Concerto in D for Flutes, oboe, horns and strings

1928   String Quartet in F major (revised 1920)
                Songs for voice and piano, on texts by Charlotte Mary
                Mew (Sea Love; Afternoon Tea; Arracombe Wood)

1929   *The Village Opera* (ballad opera in 3 acts with text and
                music by composer)

1930   *Psalm in C—The Gateway*, for chorus and small
                orchestra (text by Christopher Fry)
                Incidental Music to Flecker's *Don Juan*

1932   String Trio in B flat

1933/4	Symphony in B flat (revised in 1934)
1934	*Robin Hood* (ballad opera, dialogue by David Ayerst, lyrics by Ruth Pennyman)
1937	*A Song of Liberty*, for chorus and orchestra (text from William Blake's *The Marriage of Heaven and Hell*)
c. 1937	*Miners*, for chorus and piano (text by Judy Wogan)
1938	*Robert of Sicily* (opera for children, text by Christopher Fry, adapted from Robert Downing, music arranged by the composer)
1939	*Seven at One Stroke* (play for children, text by Christopher Fry, music arranged by composer)

(All unpublished works are held in the possession of the composer)

Published works

1934/35	String Quartet No. 1 (revised 1943)* First performed by the Brosa Quartet, London, December 1935; revised version by the Zorian Quartet, London, February 1944	20 mins.
1936/37	Sonata for Piano (revised 1942 and 1954) First performed by Phyllis Sellick, London, November 1937	21 mins.
1938/39	Concerto for Double String Orchestra* First performed by the South London Orchestra conducted by the composer, Morley College, London, April 1940	23 mins.
1939/41	Fantasia on a Theme of Handel, for piano and orchestra* First performed by Phyllis Sellick with the Walter Goehr Orchestra conducted by Walter Goehr, Wigmore Hall, London, March, 1942	16 mins.
	A Child of Our Time (oratorio for SATB soloists, chorus and orchestra, with text by composer) First performed by Joan Cross, Margaret McArthur, Peter Pears, Roderick Lloyd, London Region Civil Defence Choir and Morley College Choir and the London Philharmonic Orchestra conducted by Walter Goehr. Adelphi Theatre, London, March 1944	66 mins.

179

1941/42	String Quartet No. 2 in F sharp* First performed by the Zorian Quartet, Wigmore Hall, March 1943	21 mins.
1942	Two Madrigals, for unaccompanied chorus SATB: *The Windhover* (poem by Gerald Manley Hopkins) *The Source* (poem by Edward Thomas) First performed by the Morley College Choir conducted by Walter Bergmann, Morley College, July 1943	2 mins. 3 mins.
1943	*Boyhood's End* (Cantata on a text by W. H. Hudson, for tenor and piano) First performed by Peter Pears and Benjamin Britten, Morley College, June 1943	12 mins.
	Fanfare No. 1, for 4 horns, 3 trumpets and 3 trombones First performed at St. Matthew's Church, Northampton, September 1943	3 mins.
	Plebs Angelica, motet for double chorus First performed by the Fleet Street Choir, conducted by T. B. Lawrence, Canterbury Cathedral, September 1944	4 mins.
1944	*The Weeping Babe*, motet for soprano solo and unaccompanied chorus SATB (poem by Edith Sitwell)* First performed by Margaret Ritchie and Morley College Choir conducted by the composer, the Polytechnic, Regent St, London, December 1944	3 mins.
1944/45	Symphony No. 1* First performed by the Liverpool Philharmonic Orchestra conducted by Malcolm Sargent, Philharmonic Hall, Liverpool, November 1945	35 mins.
1945/46	String Quartet No. 3* First performed by the Zorian Quartet, Wigmore Hall, October 1946	31 mins.
1946	Preludio al Vespro di Monteverdi, for organ* First performed by Geraint Jones (before a performance of Monteverdi's *Vespers* (*1610*)), Central Hall, Westminster, November 1946	4 mins.
	Little Music, for string orchestra* First performed by the Jacques Orchestra conducted by Reginal Jacques, Wigmore Hall, November 1946	10 mins.

1946/52	*The Midsummer Marriage*, opera in 3 acts with text by the composer*	
	First performed by the Covent Garden Opera, conducted by John Pritchard, produced by Christopher West, with scenery and costumes by Barbara Hepworth and choreography by John Cranko, Royal Opera House, Covent Garden, January 1955	150 mins.
1948	*Suite for the Birthday of Prince Charles* (Suite in D), for orchestra*†	
	First performed by the BBC Symphony Orchestra conducted by Adrian Boult, November 1948	16 mins.
1950/51	*The Heart's Assurance*, song-cycle for high voice and piano (poems by Sidney Keyes and Alun Lewis)	
	First performed by Peter Pears and Benjamin Britten, Wigmore Hall, May 1951	17 mins.
1952	Dance, Clarion Air, madrigal for five voices SSATB, with text by Christopher Fry*	
	First performed by the Golden Age Singers and the Cambridge University Madrigal Society conducted by Boris Ord, Royal Festival Hall, London, June 1953	5 mins.
1953	Fantasia Concertante on a Theme of Corelli, for string orchestra*	
	First performed by the BBC Symphony Orchestra conducted by the composer, Usher Hall, Edinburgh, August 1953	16 mins.
	Fanfare No. 2, for 4 trumpets*	2 mins.
	Fanfare No. 3, for 3 trumpets	1 min.
	First performed at the St. Ives Festival of Arts, June 1953	
1953/54	Divertimento on *Sellinger's Round*, for chamber orchestra**	
	First performed by the Collegium Musicum Zürich conducted by Paul Sacher, Zürich, November 1954	16 mins.
1953/5	Concerto for Piano and Orchestra††	
	First performed by Louis Kentner and the City of Birmingham Symphony Orchestra, conducted by Rudolf Schwarz, Town Hall, Birmingham, October 1956	32 mins.

1954 Four Inventions, for descant and treble recorders*
First performed by Freda Dinn and Walter Bergmann,
Society of Recorder Players' Summer School,
Roehampton, July 1954   9 mins.

1955 Sonata for Four Horns*
First performed by the Dennis Brain Wind Ensemble,
Wigmore Hall, December 1955   20 mins.

1956 *Bonny at Morn* (Northumbrian folk-song, set for unison
voices and recorders)*
First performed at the International Pestalozzi Children's Village 10th Anniversary at Trogen, Switzer-
land, April, 1956   3 mins.

Four songs from the British Isles, for unaccompanied
chorus SATB (1. England: 'Early one morning'; 2.
Ireland: 'Lilliburlero'; 3. Scotland: 'Poortith cauld'*;
4. Wales: 'Gwenllian'.)
First performed by the London Bach Group conducted by John Minchinton, Royaumont Festival (France),
July 1958   14 mins.

1956/57 Symphony No. 2*
First performed by the BBC Symphony Orchestra,
conducted by Adrian Boult, Royal Festival Hall,
London, February 1958   32 mins.

1958 *Crown of the Year*, cantata with text by Christopher Fry,
for chorus, SSA, recorders, or flutes, oboe, cornet or
trumpet, string quartet, percussion, handbells and
piano*
First performed under the composer's direction at
Badminton School, Bristol, July 1958   28 mins.

Wadhurst, hymn tune (Unto the hills around do I lift
my longing eyes)*
Written for the Salvation Army†††
Five Negro Spirituals, from *A Child of Our Time*,
arranged for unaccompanied chorus   14 mins.

1958/61 *King Priam*, opera in 3 acts with text by the
composer***
First performed by the Covent Garden Opera, con-
ducted by John Pritchard, produced by Sam
Wanamaker and with scenery and costumes by Sean
Kenny, Coventry Theatre, Coventry, May 1962
(Coventry Cathedral Festival)   116 mins.

1960	Music, unison song for voices, string and piano, or voices and piano (poem by Shelley)* . First performed by the combined choirs of the East Sussex and West Kent Choral Festival, conducted by Trevor Harvey, Assembly Hall, Tunbridge Wells, April, 1960	4 mins.
	Music for Words Perhaps, incidental music for speaking voice(s) and chamber ensemble to a sequence of poems by W. B. Yeats First broadcast, June 1960; first concert performance, Michael Hordern, with the English Chamber Orchestra conducted by Norman Del Mar, January, 1980	14 mins.
	Lullaby, for six voices, or alto solo (or counter-tenor) and small choir SSTTB (poem by W. B. Yeats)* First performed by the Deller Consort, Victoria and Albert Museum, London, November, 1960	6 mins.
1961	*Songs for Achilles*, for tenor and guitar, with texts by the composer** (The first song appears in Act II of *King Priam*) First performed by Peter Pears and Julian Bream at the Aldeburgh Festival, June 1961	14 mins.
	Magnificat and Nunc Dimittis, for chorus SATB and organ First performed by the St. John's College Chapel Choir conducted by George Guest, March 1962	7 mins.
1962	Sonata No. 2, for piano* First performed by Margaret Kitchin, Freemason's Hall, Edinburgh Festival, September 1962	14 mins.
	Songs for Ariel, for voice and piano (or harpsichord)** (adapted from incidental music written for a production of Shakespeare's *The Tempest*, at the Old Vic Theatre, London, 1952). The songs were arranged in 1964 for an instrumental accompaniment of flute/piccolo, clarinet, horn, percussion ad lib. (bells, bass drum) and harpsichord. First concert performance by Grayston Burgess and Virginia Plesants at Fenton House, Hampstead, September 1963	5 mins.

Praeludium, for brass, bells and percussion*
First performed by the BBC Symphony Orchestra
conducted by Antal Dorati, Royal Festival Hall,
London, November 1962   6 mins.

1962/63   Concerto for Orchestra*
           First performed by the London Symphony Orchestra
           conducted by Colin Davis, Usher Hall, Edinburgh,
           August 1963   31 mins.

1963   Prelude, Recitative and Aria, for flute, oboe and piano
           (or harpsichord) (Arrangement of the third interlude
           in Act III of *King Priam*)   6 mins.

1963/65   *The Vision of St. Augustine*, for baritone solo, chorus
           and orchestra*
           First performed by Dietrich Fischer-Dieskau and the
           BBC Symphony Orchestra conducted by the composer
           at the Royal Festival Hall, London, January, 1966   35 mins.

1965/70   *The Shires Suite*, for chorus and orchestra*
           First (complete) performance by the Schola Cantorum
           of Oxford and the Leicestershire Schools Symphony
           Orchestra conducted by the composer, Cheltenham
           Festival, July 1970   18 mins.

1966   *Severn Bridge Variations* No. 6 ('Braint')† (part of a
           composite work by Arnold, Hoddinott, Maw, Daniel
           Jones, Grace Williams and Tippett)
           First performed by the BBC Training Orchestra
           conducted by Adrian Boult, Brangwyn Hall, Swansea,
           January 1967   10 mins.

1966/70   *The Knot Garden*, opera in 3 acts with text by the
           composer****
           First performed by the Covent Garden Opera conduc-
           ted by Colin Davis, produced by Peter Hall, designed
           by Timothy O'Brien and with costumes by Tazeena
           Firth, Royal Opera House, Covent Garden, December
           1970   87 mins.

1970   *Songs for Dov*, for tenor and small orchestra, with text
           by the composer**
           First performed by Gerald English and the London
           Sinfonietta conducted by the composer, University
           College Cardiff, October 1970
           (The first song appears in Act II of *The Knot Garden*)   26 mins.

184

1970/72	Symphony No. 3, for soprano and orchestra, with text by the composer* First performed by Heather Harper and the London Symphony Orchestra conducted by Colin Davis, Royal Festival Hall, June 1972	55 mins.
1971	In Memoriam Magistri, for flute, clarinet and string quartet (in memory of Stravinsky) First performed by the London Sinfonietta, June 1972	3 mins.
1972/73	Sonata No. 3, for piano* First performed by Paul Crossley, Bath Festival, May 1973	22 mins.
1973/76	*The Ice Break*, opera in 3 acts with text by the composer* First performed by Covent Garden Opera, conducted by Colin Davis, produced by Sam Wanamaker, with scenery and costumes by Ralph Koltai, Royal Opera House, Covent Garden, July 1977	75 mins.
1976/77	Symphony No. 4* First performed by the Chicago Symphony Orchestra, conducted by Georg Solti, Chicago, October 1977	32 mins.
1977/78	String Quartet No. 4 First performed by the Lindsay Quartet, Bath Festival, May 1978	23 mins.
1978/79	Concerto for violin, viola, cello and orchestra First performed by György Pauk, Nobuko Imai and Ralph Kirshbaum, with the London Symphony Orchestra conducted by Colin Davis, August 1980	31 mins.
1980	*Wolftrap Fanfare*, for 3 trumpets, 2 trombones and tuba First performed by the Brass section of the Washington National Symphony Orchestra, conducted by Hugh Wolff, at Wolftrap Farm for the Performing Arts, Vienna, Virginia, June 1980	2 mins.

SELECT DISCOGRAPHY

(NB Record numbers are all subject to change)

String Quartets 1, 2 & 3
Lindsay Quartet (L'Oiseau Lyre DSLO 10)

Piano Sonatas 1, 2 & 3
Paul Crossley (pfte) (Philips 6500534)

Symphony No. 1/Suite for the Birthday of Prince Charles (Suite in D)
LSO/Colin Davis (Philips 9500 1070)

Symphony No. 2/Sonata for 4 horns/The Weeping Babe
LSO/Davis; Barry Tuckwell Horn Quartet; John Alldis Choir (Argo ZRG 535)

Symphony No. 3
LSO/Davis (Philips 6500 662)

Symphony No. 4
Chicago SO/Georg Solti (Decca SXDL 7546)

The Midsummer Marriage
Soloists, Chorus and Orchestra of the Royal Opera House, Covent Garden/Davis (Philips 6703 027)

King Priam
Soloists, London Sinfonietta Chorus, London Sinfonietta/David Atherton (Decca D246D 3)

The Knot Garden
Soloists and Orchestra of the Royal Opera House, Covent Garden/Davis (Philips 6700 063)

186

A Child of Our Time
Soloists/Royal Liverpool Philharmonic Orchestra and Choir/John Pritchard
coupled with Ritual Dances (*The Midsummer Marriage*) (Argo DPA 571/2)
Soloists/BBC Singers/BBC Choral Society and BBC Symphony Orchestra/
Davis (Philips 6500 985)

Concerto for Double String Orchestra
Bath Festival Orchestra, Moscow Chamber Orchestra/Rudolf Barshai (HMV
SXLP 30157)
Philharmonia Orchestra/Walter Goehr (transfer of 78rpm recording) (Music
for Pleasure MFP 2069)
London Philharmonic Orchestra/Vernon Handley (Classics for Pleasure CFP
40068)

Fanfares for brass instruments
Philip Jones Brass Ensemble (Argo ZRG 870)

Piano Concerto
John Ogdon/Philharmonia Orchestra/Davis (HMV ASD 621)

Fantasia Concertante on a Theme of Corelli
Bath Festival Orchestra/Tippett (HMV ASD 637)

Orchestra of St. John's Smith Square/John Lubbock—coupled with Little
Music for Strings (Pye TPLS 13069)
Academy of St. Martin-in-the-Fields/Neville Marriner—coupled with Little
Music and Concerto for Double String Orchestra (Argo ZRG 680)

Concerto for Orchestra
LSO/Davis—coupled with Ritual Dances from *The Midsummer Marriage* (not
concert version, but taken from complete recordings of the opera) (Philips
6580 093)
Boyhood's End/The Heart's Assurance/Songs for Ariel/Songs for Achilles Philip
Langridge/John Constable/Timothy Walker (L'Oiseau Lyre DSLO 14)

Boyhood's End/The Heart's Assurance/String Quartet No. 2
Peter Pears/Benjamin Britten/Amadeus Quartet (Argo DA 34)

Songs for Ariel
Pears/Britten (Argo ZRG 5439)

The Vision of St. Augustine/Fantasia on a Theme of Handel
LSO/LSO Chorus/John Shirley Quirk/Margaret Kitchin/Tippett (RCA SER
5620)

Interlude 2 and Epilogue from *The Shires Suite*
Leicestershire Schools Symphony Orchestra/Tippett (Argo ZRG 685)

Divertimento: Sellinger's Round
ECO/Norman Del Mar (Lyrita) *in preparation*

Choral music: Dance, Clarion Air, The Source, The Windhover, Lullaby, Bonny at Morn, 4 Songs from the British Isles, Magnificat and Nunc Dimittis, Plebs Angelica, The Weeping Babe, Music, 5 Negro spirituals
Schola Cantorum of Oxford/Nicholas Cleobury (L'Oiseau-Lyre DSLO 25)

Songs for Dov
Robert Tear/London Sinfonietta/Atherton (Argo ZRG 703)

Triple Concerto, for violin, viola, cello & orchestra (Philips) in preparation

INDEX OF WORKS MENTIONED IN THE TEXT

Page numbers in *italic* denote those passages in which a work is discussed in detail.

GENERAL INDEX

Adelaide Festival 35
Adelphi Theatre 25
Akademie der Kunst, Berlin 32
Akhmatova, Anna 163–4, 166
Albee, Edward 70, 87; *Who's Afraid of Virginia Woolf?* 87
Aldeburgh 26
Allen, (Sir) Hugh 17
Allinson, Francesca 23, 27, 50
Amadeus Quartet 25
American Academy of Arts 32
Amin, Idi 44
Amis, John 24
Anderson, Ande 31
Aristophanes 56
Armstrong, Richard 36
Arne, Thomas 100
Aspen Festival 33
Auden, W. H. 56

Bach, J. S. 43; Fugue in B minor (BWV 578) 101; *St Matthew Passion* 45; *St John Passion* 45
Balzac, Honoré de 135
Barn Theatre, Oxted 19
Barrault, Jean-Louis 61
Bartok, Béla 91, 92, 97, 168
Basle Chamber Orchestra 168
Bath Festival 37, 171
Bauhaus 160
BBC 24, 26, 33
BBC Symphony Orchestra 30

Beard, Paul 30
Beethoven, Ludwig van 17, 18, 91, 92, 115, 116, 122, 123, 124, 126, 129, 158, 160; *Grosse Fuge*, Op. 133 129; *Kennst du das Land* 148; *Hammerklavier Sonata* 99, 123; Piano Concerto No. 4 in G major 90, 103–4; String Quartet in F minor, Op. 95 95; String Quartet in E flat major, Op. 127 127; String Quartet in C sharp minor, Op. 131 98; Symphony No. 9 in D minor 116, 121
Beggar's Opera, The 20
Bentley, Eric, *The Life of the Drama* 69
Berg, Alban 20
Bergmann, Walter 25
Berio, Luciano 154
Berkeley, Lennox 55
Berlin Festival 36
Berlioz, Hector, *L'Enfance du Christ* 49
Birtwistle, Harrison 70, 154
Blake, William 11, 22; *Book of Job* 48; *The Marriage of Heaven and Hell* 94; *Song of Liberty* 21
Bliss, (Sir) Arthur 55
Blue Mountain Music 81
Book of Job (Bible) 137

191